WILDPIECES

STORIES

CATHERINEHOGANSAFER

© 2015, Catherine Hogan Safer

Canada Council
for the Arts

Conseil des Arts
du Canada

Canadä

Newfoundland
Labrador

We gratefully acknowledge the financial support of the Canada Council for the Arts, the Government of Canada through the Canada Book Fund (CBF), and the Government of Newfoundland and Labrador through the Department of Tourism, Culture and Recreation for our publishing program.

Printed on acid-free paper
Layout by Tracy Harris
Cover design by Todd Manning
Cover art by Catherine Hogan Safer

Published by
KILLICK PRESS
an imprint of CREATIVE BOOK PUBLISHING
a Transcontinental Inc. associated company
P.O. Box 8660, Stn. A
St. John's, Newfoundland and Labrador A1B 3T7

Printed in Canada

Library and Archives Canada Cataloguing in Publication

Safer, Catherine, 1950-, author
Wild pieces / Catherine Hogan Safer.

Short stories.
ISBN 978-1-77103-071-7 (paperback)

I. Title.

PS8637.A44W57 2015   C813'.6   C2015-904805-2

FSC

MIX
Paper from
responsible sources
FSC® C011825

WILDPIECES

STORIES

killick press
an imprint of Creative Publishers

St. John's, Newfoundland and Labrador
2015

We are all wild
pieces of some whispering heart, moving inside light
and dark, the soles of our shoes damp
and leaking. But we move ...

from Spring again
By Lorri Neilsen Glenn,
Lost Gospels, Brick Books

PRAISE FOR *WILD PIECES*

Catherine Hogan Safer's stories are full of bold-faced, bald-eyed observation about oddballs and their antics. There is tenderness, poignancy, and 100-watt farce. Safer exposes all the human foibles with hilarity, and lashings of quirky wisdom.

– Lisa Moore
author of *February* and *Caught*

ooo

These stories are steeped in the words of children as they struggle through the world of adults. And underneath it all a spirit blooms. Hogan Safer opens the magic hinge in our lives where the rest of the world leaks in. Imagine the country songs of Bobbie Gentry mashed up on the hymns of Loretta Lynn. Funny, acerbic, tragic, gothic, fantastic, this is Newfoundland Nashville as written by the old, pre-rhinestone storytellers, of when they were young and true, when they saw the fabric of the world, beneath the glitz, as it really is.

– Michael Winter
author of *This all Happened* and *The Architects are Here*

Readers of Catherine Hogan Safer's wonderful novel, *Bishop's Road*, will not be surprised to find themselves loving her new book of stories, but they may not be expecting the variety of voices in it, the unpredictable shifts of plot, the wide range of quirky characters – many of them damaged or troubled or put-upon – and the fascinating turns taken by their lives. *Wild Pieces* swings all the way from hilarious to heart-wrenching. These crisply written, enigmatic stories never say one iota more than needs to be said. They give voice to the so-called ordinary folks who seldom find ways to speak for themselves, and they keep on percolating in a reader – at least they do in me – well after they end. Literary magic like Catherine Hogan Safer's is rare enough in the world, and to be treasured.

– Stan Dragland, Professor Emeritus, University of Western Ontario, Publisher and Editor, Brick Books

ooo

Catherine Hogan Safer's voice is so real; she makes characters and situations that could be considered unusual become authentic and understandable. I loved every word of this warm and captivating window on human nature.

– Janice Wells
author of *Frank Moores: The Time of His Life* and
The Gin and Tonic Gardener

PRAISE FOR
BISHOP'S ROAD

"Bishop's Road is a magic and moving story that eludes description... The novel heralds the talent of a very original voice. Catherine Safer has created a novel of complexity and compassion."

– Mary Jo Anderson,
The Nova Scotian

ooo

"Safer writes with authority, wit and dash. St. John's is described with a keen eye and a touch of mystery... Her style is her own, and it is sure, and poetic, with lots of humour and energy and unique phrasings."

– Joan Sullivan,
The Telegram

ooo

"In Bishop's Road, first-time novelist, Catherine Safer has composed a love song to St. John's, NL, with lyrics that would make Cole Porter, Stan Rogers – or even Ron Hynes – proud...suffused with a life-affirming wonderment that reveals the interconnectedness with the world and embraces life's eccentrics..."

– Bretton Loney,
The Daily News

"It's a ghost story for people who don't like ghost stories, a mystery for people who couldn't care less whodunit, an antidote for those who overdosed on The Shipping News."
— Robin McGrath,
The Northeast Avalon Times

ooo

"Bishop's Road is a keeper. It has the loveable characters of Maeve Binchy, the magic realism of Alice Hoffman, combined with the insightful quirkiness of Anne Tyler…one of the most memorable novels of the year."
— W.P. Kinsella,
Books in Canada

**Judges' comments, 2004 Amazon.ca/
Books in Canada First Novel Award**

"Bishop's Road jumped off the page at me, playfully rendering the stories of as colourful a bunch of women as we're ever likely to meet."
— Bill Gaston

"…an unusual book…Safer floored me with her grasp of story, character, and most particular of all, her avoidance of all the novels she didn't write…it is a tribute to the author that she ploughs her own field…a well-wrought world, this book."
— Michael Winter
author of *This all Happened* and *The Architects are Here*

TABLE OF CONTENTS

BENNY

The whole thing was probably Benny's fault. If he didn't crash into the house that time sliding and end up in the hospital with his head busted up and all those bones broken and having to lie there the rest of the winter nothing would have happened. But he did even after Mom said don't you dare go on that hill out back it's too steep one of these days someone's going to get killed and don't come running to me when you do.

The thing was you could only go there when it was dark after you had your homework done and Mom was finished doing the supper dishes and gone to sit in the living room with her cup of tea. You could say hey Mom we're going over to Jim's house his dad said we could and she'd be so tired after the day she put in her feet were killing her that she'd be glad to see us out the door but only for an hour you get back here in an hour or God help the both of you. And we'd make a big deal out of going out the front and circle round the house where we kept our toboggan and then Mike Robby Harry Glen Jim and Joanie would come over with their own sleds and toboggans except for Joanie who only ever had a bit of cardboard or the lid off a garbage can being poor and all.

The time when Benny crashed into the house and ended up in the hospital he was feeling sorry for Joanie and let her have his turn on our toboggan and that night she had the lid off of Mr. Hedley Morgan's garbage can, which she swiped on the way over, it being garbage day and he didn't take his in yet. So I suppose you could say it was all her fault what happened because she knows good as anyone that Benny's not the kind to hang out at the top of the hill doing nothing and he decided to go down on the garbage can lid. Me and Benny were never poor as such and never had to make do with cardboard or a garbage can lid as we always had at least one toboggan between us. So Benny wasn't used

3

to the speed those things can pick up, especially when the hill was basically a lump of ice from the thaw freeze thaw freeze we were after having lately. Down he goes and he couldn't stop, ran right over me and Joanie and into the corner of the house. We were being quiet so as not to disturb Mom with her cup of tea but the crack when his head hit the concrete was so loud she could hear it all the way in the living room and came tearing out.

We figured he had to be dead since he didn't move but Mom screamed out to Dad go start the car and they took him to the hospital. Me and the boys and Joanie just stood around for a while. We didn't feel so much like sliding any- more and soon they took off and Joanie brought the garbage can lid back to Mr. Hedley Morgan's place even though it had a lot of Benny's blood still on it.

I sat in the house then for about five hours waiting to hear. I was sleepy but I didn't want to go to bed. It would be too strange in my room without Benny across the hall and coming in to visit and talk for a while. I wasn't sure what I would do if he really was dead I was so used to having him around.

When Mom and Dad came home without him I started to cry and Mom hauled off and smacked me so hard across the face I thought my head was going to come clean off and she was crying too. Dad said now Edie it's not the child's fault these things happen and then he said that Benny was going to be all right but they had him in traction for his back and he was in pretty bad shape right now but things were looking good for a full recovery. Then Mom said what the hell were you thinking letting your brother go down that hill on a garbage can lid for the love of God are you out of your mind we spend a fortune on toboggans and this is what you do when my back is turned I told you not to go near that hill I told you John you've got to do something

4

about those youngsters they're driving me right around the bend.

That's when Mom started baking bread again like she used to years ago when we were little when she had more kids to feed not just two left the others grown and out on their own. The only trouble being that she didn't know how to make a couple of loaves of bread and maybe a pan of those nice rolls with the little buttery tops. No. She only knew how to make enough bread for five kids and two parents and by the time we got through a loaf and a bit with Benny getting a loaf at the hospital too that he said the nurses ate then the rest of it would be getting dry and stale tasting and nobody wanted to eat it. There was no point trying to put it in the freezer since Dad's way of thinking was bad as Mom's and he was forever buying too much food when it went on sale and they even had to buy another freezer for his bargains usually things that nobody wanted to eat anyway – chicken livers beef tongue and such. Mom would cook them up Benny and I wouldn't eat them and Dad would go on about how the older kids ate whatever was put in front of them what's wrong with the two of you. Mom would say don't be so foolish John the older ones never ate anything willingly that you liked and I'm fed up with nagging youngsters about food you two go make yourselves a sandwich and quit your complaining.

Then Benny in the hospital bored silly had the great idea of bringing some of the bread over to Mrs. Covey who lived down the road from us and had a better hill than ours. What you can do he said is start bringing her a loaf every time Mom goes baking and then after a week or so of that you should bring your toboggans with you and make like you're going to the park to slide after you drop off the bread. And you know how she gets talking whenever she has half a chance, well if say Joanie was to make a comment about hurry up let's get over to the park I got to be home before it gets dark and maybe Robby could say we shouldn't be going there anyways since a young girl was killed there once it's dangerous and Joanie could say that's why I got to be home before dark and then if Glen was to look longing at Mrs. Covey's hill and wish out loud he had something like that close to his house so he didn't have to go all the way to the park then I bet you anything Mrs. Covey would say come on in kids and slide here. Come over anytime you want.

Trouble with that idea was that Mrs. Covey never did take to us no matter how much bread we brought over. Could be she didn't even like bread and was just being polite since we always said that mine and Benny's mom was the one asked us to bring it, but that never occurred to us 'til later on. Every time Mom's back was turned I grabbed another loaf and took off to Mrs. Covey's. Mom never knew where the bread was going and she never asked. I daresay she never cared much either being worried about Benny, who the doctor said wasn't coming along as good as they first thought and would need some kind of special exercise to learn how to walk again and it would probably hurt like hell. Last going off she was baking every day, crying her heart out into the dough about Benny while she worked it and every batch was saltier than the last one, so neither me nor Dad could eat it anymore, and even the nurses who Benny said would eat anything that wasn't moving were leaving the crusts so Mrs. Covey got most of it.

It wasn't until about the start of March we found out what she was doing with all that bread. One day when we went over still hoping there was a chance she'd say come on and use my hill if you like, she came to the door with all her winter clothes on. Never said a word just snatched the bread and we walked away but Joanie had the bright idea to see where she would be going now with her coat and boots on and her old fuzzy cap, and she hid back of a snow bank and watched. Turned out she was going all the way over to the lake and feeding the ducks along with four big old swans and a goose. She lugged the bread in a pillowcase looked like, and tore it up and flung it. And then some seagulls came over too and pigeons and they all had a feast on Mom's salty bread.

We watched every day for a couple of weeks but then it got boring and we all played street hockey for the rest of the winter. Benny mended enough to come home from the hospital. Mom stopped baking bread and we went back to store bought, which me and Benny liked better anyway.

We forgot all about Mrs. Covey until they found her dead over at the lake all frozen and kept fresh from the last big storm. Nobody knew what happened, why she'd be over there so old and all and a long walk from her house, figured she must have had a heart attack or something and then it snowed on her so nobody could see her, she's so little and bent over. Me and the boys and Joanie tried to find out if maybe they found a pillowcase near Mrs. Covey's body. We asked everyone we knew and Mom looked at me kind of queer when I brought it up. They all said there was nothing in the news about a pillowcase, what in God's name would she have a pillowcase for over by the lake, go away and stop bothering me will you.

We decided those birds got so used to seeing her everyday that the last time after we didn't bring her any bread she must have gone to tell them the party was over so to speak and they didn't like that. Jumped on her and pushed her down. Sat on her until she gave up and kept warm on her little old body for a while until someone else came along with a bag of bread and by then it was snowing, heading into the big storm that covered her over until April. The only thing we can't figure out is whose fault it is.

MAEVE

Maeve put a 'Help Wanted' sign in her living room window and went outside to make sure it could be seen through the branches of the gigantic aphid-infested maple tree in the front yard. Maeve doesn't have crayons or markers or such around the house. No one has thought to provide her with grandchildren yet who might want to use them – supervised, naturally – children do have a way of messing things up – and so she made do with the last of her stash of lipstick samples from the Avon lady, and even after 40 years in a drawer, they proved bright and clear enough to read from the sidewalk.

Artie Baker, walking by a few hours later, was the first to take notice. He didn't want work really, but he needed some. Katie had been after him for weeks now to get his lazy arse off the couch. She's fed up being the only one bringing in money around here and if he didn't find a job soon he could get the hell out. She wouldn't buy another drop of beer and that she wouldn't he was on his own. And that was all she had to say about it. Not another word. Which wasn't true and she kept it up day after day until he was afraid he might do her some serious damage. Then she took his keys and told him the doors would be locked until she came home from work and maybe that would help him find something being outside all day.

He went over to the tavern and had almost convinced the bartender to give him a drink on credit when the manager happened in and turfed him out don't show your face again until you get that tab paid up. In full. At Harry's Groc and Conf he tried to get the new fellow to sell him a cigarette but not a chance. Harry would always have a pack open and sell them by the each but this friggin foreigner was sticking to the rules and he was very sorry about it but there was nothing he could do.

Artie wandered down to the waterfront. There was a cruise ship in as big as a hotel and people were getting off looking like they didn't have a care in the world. Of course they don't, thought Artie, they're friggin rich as God coming here and showing off their fancy clothes and their big watches. After an hour or so glaring at passengers – some of them wanted to take his picture, he looking so quaint and all, but they weren't willing to pay – he made his way back up over the hill. He was getting hungry and the fog was rolling in. Pecking at his heels as he climbed.

He stopped to lean on Maeve's fence for a rest. That's when he saw the sign. Like a message from God. He didn't stop to wonder what Maeve was doing putting a sign up. Huffed his way up over the stairs to the front door. Maeve, what are you at? – calling through the screen. No answer so he went on in. Maeve was having a nap on the daybed in the kitchen. She stirred and mumbled something that Artie couldn't make out so he went over to her and shook her shoulder. What are you saying, woman?

Maeve opened her eyes. Artie Baker! I thought I locked that door! What do you want?

I came in about your sign. What would you be needing help with anyway? Have you got a little business on the go or what?

No. I got no little business on the go. But one of the cats is after flicking peas under the fridge and I can't get at them. They'll be rotting and stinking up the house so I wants help moving it so I can clean.

So you got no job on the go? I figured you was looking to pay someone for something.

I'm not paying but if you give me a hand with the fridge I'll make you a bit of lunch. I got some ham if you want a sandwich and some tomato soup.

Okay. Seeing as I'm already here. And we don't need to move the fridge. You got anything long and pointy we could just poke under and scoop them peas out?

Sure I could of thought of that myself.

But you never did now, did you.

There's likely something down in the basement. Frank had a lot of old tools and things. A saw might do it. Long enough to get all the way under. Why don't you go look and I'll make your sandwich.

If it's all the same to you, Maeve, I'd just as soon have that ham fried up with a couple eggs and some toast. And if you got any tea on the go that would be nice too.

You don't want much now, do you? It's only a few peas for God's sake.

Yes. And it's only a stink if you don't get them out.

All right. Ham and eggs and toast. But you got to get every last one of them peas.

After lunch Artie was in no hurry to get going. Katie wouldn't be home from work for hours yet and then she'd just be at him again anyway. Maeve's kitchen was nice and clean. Little frilly curtains on the windows with roosters running all over and grapes. Paper napkins on the table with more little roosters. Her cupboards full. Katie usually had a mess going on with dirty dishes in the sink and the bread grainy and hard to chew.

Anything else you need done while I'm here? I got the rest of the day free if you want some heavy lifting done.

Well, now that you mention it, there's a few old branches came down in the garden that last big wind and since you got the saw out anyway you might as well cut them into a good size for the wood stove. I was thinking about going to the store for potatoes. You're welcome to have supper here if you like. Since Frank's been gone it gets kind of lonesome all by myself.

That would be grand, Maeve. If you felt like it you could pick up some cold beer too while you're out. I finds hard work makes a man thirsty.

It took all Maeve had to get Artie Baker out of the house that evening. It was nice enough having someone around and he did dry the dishes after supper but she likes to watch Jeopardy and Coronation Street and Artie won't shut up. She asked him will he please hold his comments until the commercials but he couldn't. She said it's time to go about a dozen times before he finally got out of the chair and left and then only when she said she might have a bit of work for him tomorrow.

He was back before breakfast. She fed him and tried to come up with a job that would keep him out of the way while she watched the news. In the basement were a few old pieces of furniture that Frank had been working on stripping before he went. She found sandpaper and showed Artie what to do. She had barely settled in with her knitting and CNN when he was back up over the stairs calling out that the light was gone down there and did she have a spare bulb. A hundred watts if she didn't mind – his eyes weren't what they used to be.

Ten minutes later he was looking for a cup of tea – the dust was making him thirsty. Then he needed a mask for the coughing and his lungs weren't all that good now even though he was hardly smoking anymore since Katie wouldn't give him any money these days and he couldn't find a job that paid anything. After that, Maeve locked the basement door from the top of the stairs and turned up the TV real loud so she couldn't hear him banging on it. She waited a couple of hours before checking on him but he was gone through the outside basement door.

Well, said Maeve to herself, I guess that's that, but she had just heated a can of beans for her lunch when he was back. He was smoking a cigarette and she wondered where he got the money to buy them until she remembered that Frank used to keep change in a jar from when he emptied his pockets. He always came in through the basement since Maeve couldn't abide the smell of his dirty old clothes after him being out on the oil trucks all day. He took off his uniform in the workroom and when it needed cleaning he had his own little washer. She couldn't have grease and oil in the good one getting on the sheets and towels. He probably had liquor down there too – she should have checked before sending Artie Baker down to sand the furniture.

I can finish up that work for you now, Maeve, he said, and made his way to the basement.

There's no smoking in this house, Artie Baker. You put that thing out right now.

I'll just leave the outside door open a crack, Maeve, you won't smell a thing. You got anymore of them beans left? Maybe a bit of toast?

For a full week Maeve fed Artie Baker, begging him out of her house at night. Wishing to hell he would fall off the face of the earth and leave her alone. She began keeping the curtains closed so he couldn't see in and the house was dark as a tomb. There was no point to ignoring him ringing the bell because when she didn't answer he just started banging on the back door then around to the front again every few minutes until she gave up.

She was losing sleep. She brushed her teeth with the arthritis cream. She left one of the cats out all night and it wouldn't speak to her for two days. She dropped so many stitches in the sweater she's making for her great niece that she had to start over. She forgot to watch Days of our Lives twice and doesn't know what's going on anymore. She can't find where she put the kettle and has to boil water in a saucepan for her tea. On day seven of Artie's invasion she left the house for a couple of hours after not getting him any lunch and came home to find he had helped himself and left a mess all over the counters.

She was at the point of calling the police to come take him when Katie showed up late one night. She thought it might be Artie back again. When Maeve peeked and saw who it was she let her in. Katie asked her was she keeping Artie here deliberately or was he driving her crazy all by himself. Maeve began to cry and Katie said I'll make tea. Maeve told her to use a saucepan since she didn't know where the kettle was. Katie found it in a cupboard when she went looking for sugar.

I have to tell you, girl, said Katie, when I first noticed, I thought to myself, thank God. Finally. He was coming home later and later and not even hungry. Just going up to bed out of it. Then I got curious. Not that I give a damn. It was such a relief to have the evenings to myself and not having to listen to him, and look at him, big old slug snoring on the couch. Not having to hide my purse away. I haven't had to go out for groceries for a full week.

But I asked around and Doris O'Leary told me she thought he was coming over here. Well I tell you, at first I was good with it but then I started feeling guilty. I've always liked you, Maeve. Our kids used to play together and all and I can't think how much time we spent drinking tea and yammering when they were little. It's sad we lost touch over the years but you know I think the world of you still. I can't let Artie make you crazy. Unless, she said, hopefully, you like having him here?

No, cried Maeve. I needed a few peas out from under the fridge and he was the only one came in about my 'Help Wanted' sign. I would've got Michael over but him and Jane are off to France for a holiday. They won't be home for another week. And you know my other two moved to Alberta. There was no one to ask except Peter next door but he went and broke his leg. The new people on the other side don't seem all that friendly yet so I couldn't ask them.

Katie stared at Maeve while she sobbed and talked, thinking that peas would simply dry up and what was the panic. Wondered what might be lurking under her own fridge. Shook her head hard and carried on.

Well, Maeve, it's time to get him out of here. You look like you could crack any minute. Trouble is, I really don't want him back at my place either.

But he's your husband, cried Maeve. You have to take him. Don't you?

See, that's the thing, said Katie. We aren't exactly married. I know, everyone thinks we are. Seemed easier than explaining different. After John died I was lonely. The kids are grown and gone. When Artie came along I was feeling pretty low. John didn't have much in the way of insurance and it wasn't easy making ends meet. I had started a job that I didn't like. Artie was doing well – so he said. He was almost good looking and he made me laugh. I needed a laugh. John was sick for such a long time – I was worn right out. I should have had my eyes opened. I didn't. It was only later I remembered how he never seemed to pay for anything. We never went out to dinner – he was all the time praising my cooking and saying there wasn't a restaurant in town could compare. What a load of shit. It wasn't a month before he moved in to my place, and it's been four long years.

Maeve interrupted, but can't you just tell him to leave?

No. If we were married I could divorce him. But you can't divorce someone who is only living there. Like a roommate or something. Besides, do you really think that telling Artie to leave would accomplish anything?

What am I going to do, cried Maeve. He won't go away. And if you don't want him … Maybe we could say he's one of them stalkers. Tell the police.

That probably wouldn't work, Maeve. You do let him in, after all.

He won't stop banging on the doors. I don't know what else to do. It's not like I can shoot him. Can I shoot him, Katie?

No, Sweetie, you can't shoot him. Recalling why she and Maeve lost touch. The woman is an idiot. But we can come up with something if we think about it hard enough.

Maybe I could take out one of them retraining orders on him like people get sometimes, you know, when someone bothers them too much.

Well that's not a bad idea, Maeve. If you go to the police and tell them that Artie won't stop banging on your door day and night they might be able to do that. It's called a 'restraining order', actually. Tell them you want a 'restraining order'.

Can you come with me, Katie? I want to go right now. I can't take another minute of this arressment.

That would be 'harassment', Maeve, and, sure, let's go now. Might as well get it over with. Though I really hate the thought of that fool back at my place. I'm just getting comfortable.

It's a lovely night. Katie and Maeve walk over to the police station to see about getting Artie out of at least one of their lives. Of course, there is no one about but for the woman at the front desk. It's midnight she tells them. Best come back and talk to someone in the morning. I'm just here to answer emergency calls and get the officers out to check on them.

Well this is an emergency, cries Maeve. Artie Baker won't leave me be and I want to get him a retraining order.

Restraining order, says Katie. Restraining order!

Oh, says the woman at the front desk, that's different. There's violence involved then. And Mr. Baker is a family member?

Well, no, says Katie. He's nobody's family member that we know of and he's not violent – wouldn't hurt a fly really – he's too lazy. Maeve just wants him to leave her alone and go home. She explains the situation – beginning with the peas under the fridge, and wondering what the hell she is going on about. Maeve starts to sob a little – for effect perhaps.

Oh for God's sake! The woman at the front desk stares for a full minute before standing and clearing her throat. Says they should go away and stop wasting her time and don't bother coming back in the morning. What they have is a case of stupid. Stupid to be opening the door to another stupid and stupid to be getting involved with stupid and coming to the stupid police station with more stupid. You think you've got problems? You wouldn't know a problem if it up and bit you. I can't believe the shit I have to put up with around here. Every friggin night there's some ass coming in thinking we can solve their stupid stupid stupid. That's all it is, you know. Stupid. You, stupid, stick a sign out and let stupid in. Serves you right. What the hell were you thinking? Wait a minute! You weren't thinking, were you? And you know why? Because you're stupid. Peas are just going to dry up anyway. Christ!

Katie walks behind the glass partition and gives the woman at the front desk a hug. Pats her on the back making little 'there, there' sounds. You do realize that we are probably going to report you to your boss for this, right?

Good. My name is Tess White. Can you do the report right away? The sooner they see it, the sooner I'll get the boot. Seriously. You can use this computer if you want. Pointing at the front desk – I'll make sure the printer is turned on. Just delete your document when you're done. I don't want them thinking I did it myself. And you'll probably have to come in after they see it and go through the whole story again. Make a copy for yourself so you don't forget anything.

Tess White shuffles through a file and comes up with a piece of paper. Here's the address of the guy in charge of complaints. Put in that I hit your stupid friend there, it will carry more weight.

Katie asks, are you out of your mind?

Not yet. But if I have to put up with the likes of you two much longer, I will be. I hate the lot of you. Bitching and whining about every little ache and pain. I only took this job to get out of the house but I think I'll take up knitting instead. I wanted to be a cop when I was younger but I went and waited too long. Now I'm old. Figured that working here would get me close to the action but all I get to see is this kind of crap – every bloody shift. God!

Why haven't you quit if it's as bad as all that?

I'm after telling everyone I know what a great job it is. Interesting. My friends thought I was insane to do it. My husband left me a ton of money when he died. I haven't worked a day in twenty-five years. Didn't even have kids to take up my time. As far as they were concerned I should just do a bit of volunteering – sit on a few committees to restore this and erect that. Go to lunch with them and join their bloody book clubs. Now that would drive me right off the deep end. If I quit, they can all say 'I knew it' and I'll be eating crow for the rest of my days. But if I get fired they'll likely leave me alone. Especially if it's for a great reason. In fact, they'll probably never want anything to do with me again. Put in that I hit her really hard. Maybe a black eye – broken nose.

I can't lie.

Why not? Everybody does it. You wouldn't believe the shit I hear.

Maeve had been sitting on a faux leather chair in the lobby, listening for a while, nodding off. Now she is inspecting the plants. Yanking off a dead leaf here – testing the soil for dryness there. Checking for aphids. Wondering if it would be okay to take a few clippings of the Swedish ivy to root at home. She decides to ask the woman behind the desk.

Oh for the love of God! Take the whole damn thing why don't you? In fact, take all of them. And she darts out of her enclosure to start uprooting plants – flinging them every which way. How about this one? I'll help you haul it home. Take my keys. Bring my car around. It's the black BMW in the staff parking section. And she throws her purse at Maeve who has begun to cry in earnest.

Katie has had just about enough of this. She steps toward Tess White and slaps her hard across the face. Stop that! Calm yourself down! To which Tess White replies, don't you dare tell me 'calm yourself down'! I hate that! and whacks Katie over the head with the root end of a sad-looking yucca. There are leaves and dirt from hell to breakfast. Tess White sits down in the rubble and sighs. Rubs her cheek where Katie had landed her blow.

From the big front door comes a knock. Then a pounding when the officer outside gets a look at the damage in the lobby. Tess White goes to her desk behind the glass and pushes a button to let him in.

What is going on here?

None of your damned business, says Tess White.

It's really hard to tell anymore, says Katie.

Maeve is still crying. I just wanted some peas out from under the fridge.

Tess White yells, shut up about those fucking peas.

21

To the young officer, I'm leaving and I won't be back. Let someone know. She starts gathering the odds and ends that fell out of her purse when she tossed it to Maeve. Looking at Maeve and Katie, who is picking the last of the yucca dirt from her hair, she asks do they need a ride – she's going downtown for a drink but she'd be glad to give them a drive home unless they'd rather go for a drink as well in which case they are welcome to come along.

That's not a bad idea, says Katie. Come on, Maeve. They head out through the heavy glass doors. Katie calls shotgun.

JANE

Jane discovered the fine art of complaining when she wrote to the soup company about the lack of noodles all of a sudden – wanting to know why, especially since the price had gone up and the cans gotten smaller. The soup company shipped out a full case of the stuff. The cans still small and the noodles barely there but Jane sold it to her friends and bought raffle tickets with her earnings. She won a turkey and a Christmas basket filled with chutneys and cheeses and special meats in little tins. Crackers and biscuits and fruit. All wrapped in red cellophane with a green bow. She keeps the basket on the coffee table, though without the fruit and cheese once they started smelling up the house. Now and then she takes the bow off and irons it so it looks as fresh as new after 20 years.

For the longest time she received all kinds of good stuff. Cases of pop when she found a flat one and wrote away about it. The biggest bag of flour after there was a bug in the small one she bought. Tinned peaches, corn, pears. Cereal. Oftentimes she didn't even buy what she wanted. Just wrote away and said she thought the toothpaste tasted bad or the tuna fish was off.

Lately though, nobody was feeling very guilty about their substandard products and you'd be lucky to get an apology, let alone something to shut you up. And you had to bring back what you had, so the store could see proof that you had a legitimate complaint. And if the chicken was off they might give you another package and if you opened that one to make sure it was okay they'd get all pissy with you and say sure you can't be doing that. And Jane would say if it's bad no one will want it and if it's good I'll take it. What's your problem anyway?

She liked the raffles and contests best. Anything that cost $2 or three for $5 she'd buy. Once there was a trip to Cuba for her and a friend, which was a bit of a pain since she was hoping for second prize – a twenty-minute shop-

ping spree at the grocery store of her choice – and for going
that far a person needed a passport, which Jane didn't have
at the time. The rules were you couldn't sell the prize so
she went. It wasn't too bad. She stayed in the hotel and
took pictures of the different people – they were all shapes
and sizes and colours – and the meals which she thoroughly
enjoyed – her room – and even the pool, but only from her
balcony. There was no way she was going near that thing
so unnatural looking and probably warm too.

She brought Raymond with her. He was fifteen at the
time and raring to go. It was all she could do to keep him
in the hotel with her and he sulked a lot, especially looking
out the window at all those pretty girls with hardly a stitch
on.

He wasn't easy to live with. Too much like his father –
always chasing skirts as they say. She caught him once –
up in her own bedroom with some young chippie – half
naked and going at it like there was no tomorrow. When
she asked him why he didn't at least have the decency to
use his own room for his dirty business he had the nerve to
tell her it wasn't fit to sleep in let alone bring company.
Said the stupid velvet quilt freaked him out and the wall-
paper with all those clowns all over. And the lamps with
their pink shades. It wasn't a fit room for a fella.

It was soon after that he ended up in trouble. Stunned
thing decided to rob a house and sell the stuff. Picked the
nicest place in town and took everything he could carry.
DVD player and one of those skinny TV sets you put on
the wall. And all the silverware that someone's granny
must have had for a thousand years it was that battered.
He put up a note at the grocery store and the bingo hall
saying what he had and the price he wanted for it. Too bad
the people he robbed had an old aunt visiting who liked to
play bingo. When they saw the 'for sale' note they just

phoned him up and told him to bring it back or they were getting the cops. Of course he said go ahead, and they did.

He was in the young offenders' place for three months but the only thing he got there was determined to go do it again. He said it wasn't any different than buying raffle tickets as far as he could see, except that he didn't have to pay anything. Jane pointed out that being locked up was paying though she was happy enough to have the digital camera he stole, which is what she took all the Cuba pictures with. She'd still have it too but she couldn't stand to keep it on the strap. It reminded her of when Raymond's father used to try to choke her sometimes with his necktie, and it fell into the water when she was leaning over the bridge to take a picture of some whales – which weren't whales after all – just some rocks with waves crashing off them far in the distance.

LILY

For some reason Lily wanted a new address book and feeling affluent bought a pretty leather-bound contraption with space for web pages and email info and birth dates. Lots of room and the paper is pure and crinkly, the way Psalms might be if you were checking them out in the Bible belonged to your great grandmother.

She poured herself a cold beer and took the cap off a good pen. Sat comfortable to begin again. And in the old book she scratched out the names of the people of whom she hadn't heard tell in a year or more, not even a Christmas card and she's pretty sure she sent them one. And business associates because she never liked most of them anyway and since she left that life there's really no need to hang on. And then the people she owes money and has for years. Scratched them out. And dentists and doctors who moved and she hasn't found replacements. Names she couldn't put a face to if her life depended on it. Gone. And family, she has memorized all she wants to know about their wherefores and whys.

And then the dead. The lovely dead. Circled them in purple crayon that happened to be in the top drawer of the desk where she was sitting. Would she have gone looking for one if it hadn't been close to hand? She'll never know. She likes to think she would but doubts it. Around the insane she drew flower petals in yellow.

She went all the way to the XYZs – where few ever need to go – just in case and when she was done there was no one left but the young fellow who hauled away the asphalt last year when she tore up the driveway.

Her heart did not break exactly, but there was a sharp tearing right through the centre of it. Audible. Well now, she said to herself, but she got another beer and carried on. She cut out the dead and the mad – neatly – and burned them in her ashtray. One by one so as not to rush them away. She put their remains in an envelope and went to answer the telephone. It was someone looking for Amy and he argued for a while when she told him there was no one here by that name. Said he's coming over anyway and that bitch had better be packed and ready by the time he gets there. Lily called him an asshole and hung up.

Then a little girl came to the door selling chocolate bars so her brother could go to music camp for a week and learn how to play his flute better than he can now. Lily asked why he wasn't soliciting. The girl said he was shy. Standing out just past the sidewalk. He was a lot bigger than her but had no balls. That's what she said, saucy thing.

By the time Lily got back to her project one of the cats had pounced on the envelope and shaken it wild about the room. Her mad dead friends were scattered all over and she had to vacuum.

DORA

She says I am going to build myself a little rag room in the basement. There between the washer and the oil tank. Away from the pool of water that comes under the door when the rain is hard. To shut me in and the junk out. She has a lot of junk. There is a big table by the window. A good window. When the sun is low this time of year it casts nice light on her paper. A shadow behind her pen.

She finds old quilts that nobody wants any more at the thrift store. Perhaps their owners moved and couldn't be bothered to take them along. Perhaps they are in Arizona now, away from the cold where a quilt would be a silly thing to have. Perhaps they died and their kids said what on earth did they keep these for? Every goddamn quilt Mom ever made and they with only the one bedroom. Perhaps they couldn't see the fine stitching. The way the pieces were so carefully placed to make beautiful patterns.

She washes the quilts and mends where they have worn a little. She finds long wooden dowels at the hardware store, and hooks to fasten them to the ceiling. Curtain rings with clips to hang the quilts around her like a womb. And she can hear the clothes washing and the furnace warming but not the telephone or the doorbell or anyone calling out from the top of the stairs.

The table is covered with odds and ends. Beer bottles she takes to the recycling place. Garbage she throws away. Everything else she pushes to the end of the table away from her. There is a wooden egg painted with flowers that someone gave her to hold in her hand. A bag of Mason jar lids and a little box carved from a piece of tree – root, looks like – only big enough to fit a few rings or a gold chain. There is a leather elbow patch off an old wool sweater. Two boxes of matches and a metal thing that was in the stove drawer when she moved in and she doesn't know what it's for. Still, there is space enough for her coffee and an ashtray. Paper. She scrubs the table and sits to write.

She remembers a dream. In it she is walking through dark rooms, and rags hang from the ceiling. Not nice rags like her quilts – ugly rags – used-to-be-white-now-grey rags. Tattered and moving but there is no wind. She is looking for something. Pushing the rags aside as she goes room to room and the floor is stumbly like thick fog. She is looking for a baby in a crib. A baby in a crib. But when she finds the crib there is no baby though she can hear her crying. Sometimes there are cats in the crib. Dead cats. Tiny kittens. Once there was a tiger cub. She hasn't had that dream for a long time now but she sees it again like yesterday.

For three days she sits to write. For three days there is nothing but the dream. She takes her rag room apart. She folds the lovely old quilts and puts them in the cedar chest upstairs in her bedroom. The curtain rings in a little box to store in the linen closet. The dowels she stands in a basement corner. They will be good to climb runner beans in the spring. She unscrews the big hooks and places them on a shelf over the paint cans, with the nails and other odds and ends.

The dream has woven itself into the quilts. At night it creeps out of the cedar chest. Tangles itself in the bedclothes and her hair. She washes the quilts in hot water, knowing they might shrink but what else can she do? She hangs them on the clothesline for a week and lets the cold air and rain and snow work their magic. When they are dry she puts them back in the cedar chest.

Instead of weakening, the dream has become stronger. She borrows a fire bowl from her neighbour over the fence who only ever uses it to get rid of his old Christmas trees and branches that fall in the big winds. She clears her way through the snow to the back of the garden. She cuts the quilts into pieces – one by one – and burns them. When she is finished the dream is almost gone. It has a little strength at the bottom of the garden but gets weaker and weaker on the path to the house. By the time she is in the kitchen she can barely feel it at all.

She digs out a box of her children's old toys – they are long grown and don't want them anymore – and puts them in the cedar chest where the quilts had been. Bears and doggies and two lions. Soft dolls from the cabbage patch. A striped kitty. They have been hugged and kissed a thousand times, but she loves them once more before closing the lid.

FROGS

I want a frog so I dug a small pond out back of the house. Over there. Near the bugleweed. I lined it with black plastic like it said in the book and threw in some round stones that I pinched from the beach. First I put them through the dishwasher to get rid of the ocean salt. I'm pretty sure frogs don't care for salt.

Old missus next door plants mothballs every spring. Nothing ever comes of them but a terrible smell. I asked her why she does that but she can't hear me and goes on about something altogether different. And on. And on. I go inside to cook breakfast or do a little telephone banking. Check email. Make a batch of cookies. When I come back out she's still at it. She's 87 one day and 93 another. Can't make up her mind.

There are no frogs in this neighbourhood that I can see. Maybe the smell of mothballs keeps them away, but the cats drink the water in my small pond and every now and then there's a dead mouse floating belly up. It's probably the easiest way to do yourself in if your paws are too tiny to fashion a noose.

When I was a child – not here, somewhere else – there was a frog pond up behind our street. That's what we called it but I don't remember ever seeing a frog there. My brothers used to bring home buckets of tadpoles and they said that's where they got them but I've heard more than a few lies out of their mouths. My mother would make them take the tadpoles back but I'm not so sure they did. I tried following once but they were good runners and lost me somewhere over by the witchdoctor rock where the big girls used to go in the dark and put on makeup and kiss boys. Light candles and cast spells on stupid little kids like me.

It wasn't really a pond anyway just a big old hole that the bulldozers tore out of the trees and bushes to make way for another street someday and the water collected there

41

when they left and the grass grew up again and the butter-
flies came. Mosquitoes. Damselflies. It was probably a good
thirty years later that they decided to build that new street
so they needn't have been in such a rush to dig and maybe
if they hadn't, that papergirl wouldn't have gone through
the clearing on her way home that time and got herself
killed by whoever was hanging around and waiting to take
her money. Run away and no one every found out who did
it. And then of course the rest of us had to suffer for that
with our mothers all worried, keeping an eye on us and saying be back here as soon as the street lights come on and
not a minute later which wasn't so bad on a fine evening
but if it was either bit cloudy the damn things would be on
early and we'd all trudge home picking at each other for no
reason other than we had to leave what we were doing until
tomorrow.

If Dad was working the evening shift Mom would let us
play statues and flashlight in the backyard as long as we did-
n't go near your father's flowers or he'll have you killed and
don't bring every youngster on the street home with you.
One friend each and that's it.

A frog found my father's garden once and set himself up
behind a great big boulder under the mountain ash which I
called dogberry tree before I learned different. A big old
mean looking fellow that croaked all evening and slept the
rest of the time. I don't know why he decided to live with
us. It's not like we needed him or anything. My father used
more DDT than anyone before or after, and that frog served
no purpose. I want one for my garden to eat the slugs because I know they do that very well, and I don't know where
to find a hedgehog.

HENRY

Henry kept his collection in the basement near the furnace, same place there was the explosion that time when his dad was making wine and it got too warm and blew up and glass went everywhere. It happened in the middle of the night when Henry was asleep in his little bed in the same room as the furnace, and he woke up covered with glass and red wine. He can still smell it on his skin where the tiny scars are from the cuts. His arms were outside the blanket when it happened and one side of his face was showing. That's where the thin lines are still – purple in the cold and red on hot days.

After the wine blew up Henry called out to his dad to tell what happened but his dad must have been asleep and didn't hear. The door to the kitchen was locked on the other side and Henry couldn't open it so he washed the blood off his arms and face at the laundry sink and went back to his bed. In the morning when his dad opened the door and called him up for school he said there was no way the wine exploded all by itself and Henry must have broken the bottles with a stick or something. Henry said he would never do that but his dad didn't believe him and sent him to school with no breakfast.

When Henry came home for lunch he had to clean up where the wine was, and the glass, and there was no time to eat. He was very hungry by supper and he can remember to this day that his dad had cooked pork chops and mashed potatoes and green peas. Henry hated green peas but he wasn't allowed to leave the table until he'd eaten all of them. His dad cooked green peas every day. He said that the more Henry ate them the more he would learn to like them but it never happened.

When Henry's mom left, she took Henry's little sisters who were five and four and three years old. Henry was seven at the time. Henry's dad told her she could take those youngsters as far as she wanted and she said not Henry. He looks more like you than you do and if I had to see that face every day I'd probably smash it. He can stay with you. Henry's dad argued with her for one full night but she still said no, she didn't want Henry. Henry listened to them fighting until his little sisters woke up and started crying and he had to go sit in their room and sing to them so they wouldn't be afraid. The next day his mom took his little sisters away in her car and they waved good-bye.

After the wine blew up and Henry had all those lines on his face he thought she might be able to look at him again since he wasn't so much like his dad anymore on one side. He asked his dad if he could call and maybe go see her. His dad gave him the phone number and said knock yourself out, kid. Henry could hear his little sisters in the background before his mom told him to go to hell, and hung up.

Henry grew, and worked hard in school. His teachers told him he was smart and not to let the other students bother him too much about his scars and his quiet ways. They gave him books to take home and he read them at night in his little bed. His dad taught him how to use his fists so that when the other kids picked on him he could hold his own. Once he had to punch a guy who tripped him and shoved him into a mud puddle, took his backpack and dumped everything out all over the ground. He had to beat up a girl who was hurting another girl, pulling her hair out, and her nose was bleeding. The girl he saved followed him home even though he asked her not to, and told his dad what Henry did for her. Henry's dad gave him a sound whack upside his head for hitting a girl. Henry stopped defending after that – himself or anyone else.

The girl who had followed him home tried to be his friend for a long time. She was an ugly little thing named Alice and she was in Henry's class all through school. She was smart like Henry, but dirty, and the other children were mean to her. She smelled like bacon fat and damp clothes. She had sores on her arms and face and someone made up a story about her having leprosy so no one would sit near her. Miss Jones said there was no such thing as leprosy anymore. Alice wouldn't let things heal, was all. She scratched and scratched and if she didn't stop it soon she'd be nothing but a giant scab and Miss Jones said at that rate she'd never find a husband and even the nuns wouldn't have her.

When Henry graduated from high school, his dad told him he had to learn a trade. No son of his was going to university to be a friggin doctor or lawyer or anything else that wanted more money than he was willing to spend.

Henry's teachers tried to convince his dad that Henry had a wonderful future, could do anything he put his mind to, and Henry's dad said no again. They helped him apply for every scholarship available and he came up with enough to get him started but his dad still said no. Henry was sent to the community college to learn how to be a plumber. If it was good enough for Henry's dad it was good enough for Henry.

Henry's dad said a man was only worth what he could do with his own two hands. Henry wanted to point out that doctors use their hands all the time, especially if they are surgeons, but he didn't. He learned how to be a plumber like his dad and as soon as he finished college and found work, his dad decided it was time to retire while he was young enough to enjoy life and it was Henry's turn to earn a living for both of them.

Henry had started his collection just after the wine blew up. He took a box of matches from his dad's jacket pocket and placed it under the pillow on his little bed in the basement near the furnace. His dad was angry when he couldn't find anything to light his cigarette and made Henry go to the store even though it was winter stormy out and Henry could hardly make his way through the drifts because he was still little and his legs not very long.

After the matches, he took one of his dad's grey wool socks that his own mother had made for him, God rest her soul. And her fingers were arthritic, but still she knitted away for her darling son. I know you took that sock, Henry. Where the hell did you put it? And Henry said he didn't know where it was, but he did. That night Henry's dad didn't cook anything for Henry. Opened a can of peas and told him to eat them cold. The next week Henry took the other sock.

For a long time Henry collected little bits and pieces of his dad. His good shirt. His new magazine. A toothbrush. Hair from his comb. When his dad threw away old shoes, Henry dug them out of the garbage. He never took more than a few things in the run of a year. When he knew his collection was complete he laughed. I have enough to build another dad he said, but there was no one listening.

Henry's dad decided he might as well go out and find a woman for himself. Not that he ever again wanted a wife but he could use some company now and then. For the first time in his life, Henry was alone in the house at night. His dad went out after supper and didn't come home until all hours. Henry still had to stay in the basement in the room with the furnace and the lock on the door to the upstairs but there was no one to yell down at him and ask what he was doing if he made a sound. He took wood, hammer, nails and a saw from his dad's workshop. Henry's dad no longer had use for them since the time he broke his arm and it didn't heal very well. Henry built a little coffin.

Henry's job was at a new housing development where fancy big homes were being built for people with money. He spent his time installing pipes and bathroom fixtures.

His co-workers usually went away from the site for lunch but Henry brought sandwiches and coffee in a thermos. Once, he began working again before the others returned and they gave him a hard time about it. Called him a suck up and brown nose and who did he think he was trying to impress anyway.

A little way beyond the new development was leftover forest that hadn't been torn up yet and Henry decided to have his lunch there. He could listen to birds and there was a little river. Henry found it peaceful like nothing he had ever felt before. It made him sad but happy all at the same time. One day he walked further than usual and came upon a small house. A fairy tale house, thought Henry. Gingerbread? And Henry laughed to himself for being silly. He looked around for three bears and laughed again. It's a wonderland he said, and thought of Alice with the scabs and the dirty smell and how he had saved her that day when she was being hurt. Henry stopped laughing.

Henry couldn't remember the last time he had cried and the sound that came out of him along with the tears was shocking, though the ache was familiar, was always with him, but not wet and salty and didn't make his nose run like this crying did. What is wrong with me, he said, sitting on a rock and bawling like a baby at the sight of a shabby little house in the scrappy woods.

After Henry had been crying for a long time, a dog came by. Smallish with floppy ears – wagging its whole body to make up for no tail. It put its front paws on Henry's knees and licked the tears from Henry's face and ran away.

Henry thought of something he read once, about elephants, how they were captured sometimes when they were little and chained by their legs to posts for a long time. And how, when they grew up, and the chains were taken away, they stayed put, like they forgot they could go anywhere they wanted. And he remembered thinking they must be pretty stupid.

Henry didn't go back to work. He went home to his room in the basement. He put all of his dad's things that he had taken over the years into the little coffin and nailed it shut. He found a screwdriver and removed the lock from the upstairs kitchen door. Then he removed the door itself, and placed it on his father's bed.

MARTHA

At three in the morning Martha decides to paint the house blue. Not a pale blue like watered down sky. A large blue. Like the ocean in a good mood. Calm. She calls Mike right away and tells him what she is going to do.

He says why don't you wait until I get home?

She says but that will be another three weeks.

He says send me the colour samples then, and I'll call Jim. If he's not too busy we can hire him to do it. I don't see how on earth you could manage it.

It's not that big a deal. We have a ladder. It's not like I've never painted anything before. Remember the baby's room? I did a good job with that, Mike.

Yes you did, sweetheart. You really did. But Martha, that was a small room, not an entire house. We'll get Jim to do it. He's got a big crew. It will only take a few days.

But Jim won't be available this time of year. He always says that summer he doesn't have a minute to spare.

Please, Martha. The storm windows will have to come off. And we might as well have them cleaned when they're down. And there are a few pieces of clapboard to be replaced. There's no way you can handle that on your own. It's a huge job. Be reasonable, darling.

What are you talking about, Mike? And she realizes that he thinks she means the outside of the house. Okay, she says. Never mind.

Martha, we can have it done. I like the idea of a blue house. I really do. Just wait until I get home.

But Martha has hung up.

As soon as the hardware store opens Martha buys ten gallons of steel blue paint. High gloss. The clerk asks if she's planning to paint the whole town and laughs.

And if I am? How is that your business? She smiles so he will know that she is really a nice person. Just kidding around friendly like. And she keeps the smile on her face until she realizes he isn't going to help load the paint into her car.

At home Martha asks where do I begin? Of the cat. Of the stove. Of the spider on the kitchen window weaving her thin thin web. At the top and work down, I think that's best. And she paints the upstairs bathroom first. Walls. Ceiling. Tub and toilet. Sink and vanity. Floor. I always hated that floor. Dreary. And that house across the street with mister always taking his clothes off with the curtains open. Looking over here to see if I'm watching. She paints the window. Bedrooms next. Linen closet. Landing and stairs. She's tired now and hungry but if she stops she will lose her momentum. It sometimes takes Martha a long time to get going but when she does she's like a house on fire. She can't stop. Maybe after she does the living room. The dining room.

She moves the window spider with the thin thin web to the garden. It is a wild and evil place. Overgrown with weeds and you could never tell that it had once been pretty with hundreds of different flowers. Since the baby, Martha hasn't gone out there at all. She puts the spider on a patch of goldenrod and paints the kitchen.

At midnight she gets in the car and goes to the chicken take-out a few streets over. Missy at the counter says what are you doing, painting?

No, says Martha. I'm turning blue. But she smiles to let the girl know she's only kidding and orders a lot of food. Some for the cat too. Extra napkins, please.

There is no ketchup for her fries because she has painted the fridge shut. Well that's a bitch, she says, and after telling the girl she didn't need condiments. I guess I was lying. Martha goes back to the take-out which is now closed to business and no one will answer her banging on the door.

In the basement pantry, which hasn't been painted yet,

there is a jar of mango chutney which will have to do and isn't so bad, Martha decides, on chicken and fries. She tears meat off bones for the cat and he is content to sit with her on the backyard deck and dine. When they are finished she cleans the cat's blue feet with water from the outside tap and the extra napkins. Then her own body – face and arms. Legs.

They sleep curled together in the warm and sticky night air. Martha tells the cat that there is no way the paint will ever dry in this humidity. Maybe we should have waited until the weather cools.

MADONNA

If Mom didn't have so many kids everything would have been okay, but as it is she went and had the six of us and wore herself right out. At least that's the way I see it. If it was just me we'd be happy – her and me – and none of this would've happened. She told me she loved me best. Couldn't stand the others. Said if she had any sense she'd have drowned the lot of them before they even had their eyes opened. I'm the only one takes after her. We're skinny and taller than the rest; they're like Dad. Kind of normal looking — not too long, not too thin.

Dad was a pain she said — friggin Catholic getting her pregnant every time she turned around. And in this day and age too, when nobody cared anymore if people used birth control, not even the Pope. She went on the pill once, she told me, but he found her stash and gave her a smack and after that she had the twins. At least they didn't come along one close after the other like the girls. I was six and my sisters were seven and eight and nine when the boys came.

Dad was proud of us, I have to say. He was forever taking pictures. He carried us around in his wallet — six individual photos and a group shot. As soon as the leaves came out on the big maple at the end of the lawn, it was line up short to tall — by the trunk — and don't step on that new patch of grass or I'll kill the lot of you. Summertime behind his precious roses no matter how many aphids were crawling all over us — line up short to tall and don't you lay a finger on those flowers. Now shut up and smile. And at Christmas, after he went overboard decorating the house. Line up short to tall and stop your bawling — Davey was always upset about something — or I'll give you something to really screech about. Now smile, for the love of God, so I can get this over with. Didn't matter how old we were, it was always short to tall.

We had special outfits for the pictures. Red dresses with white collars for the girls. Blue shirts and black pants for the boys. And we always had to have our shoes shined so we could see in them. We only ever got to rig out like that for the pictures and for very special occasions. As soon as he finished, Dad would be yelling go change right now so you don't get dirty. At midnight mass he made us take our coats off so people could see how nice we looked. We dressed up for Christmas day too, but he always said if we got so much as a hint of gravy on something we'd have to leave home right now.

Over the years, we got to be looking pretty ratty all the same. Dresses always being traded. Mom would make new ones when anyone's got too small, but she wasn't so great at sewing — or washing things out for that matter — and the reds turned into pinks and pale purples.

My sisters had it easy, being a sensible height, but the only dress ever fitted me was the first one when I was about five. After that I was too thin for the ones handed down. Dad would make fun of me and I was always at the tall end after I got to be eight. Whatever I wore was too short and had to be pinned in the back to make it even half-way fit. Molly was forever pinching my arms too, so there's a lot of pictures of me in the world looking real pathetic.

Last going off, Molly decided she wasn't going to wear a dress. I remember she said screw this crap and turned up in jeans and a t-shirt and the sneakers she wore for playing softball. She knew Dad was drunk even though she swore up and down that she didn't, but I know she never would've done that if he wasn't drinking, no matter how brave she thinks she is. Dad gets kind of sissy and sad when he has more than a few drinks and sometimes he ends up crying and kissing everyone.

That was the year none of the pictures got developed.

They stayed curled up in the camera in Katie's dresser drawer. I found it when I went looking for something. It might still be there.

I used to sleep in a room with all three of my sisters — Katie and Molly and Bridget. We had bunk beds and two dressers that we shared. They didn't like me. I'm pretty sure because Mom loves me best.

When Joey and Davey were finally in school all day, Mom started to lose it. She was probably too busy up to that point to think about anything other than us. With nobody in the house after breakfast, she didn't have enough to do. That's what I figure, anyway.

First she had it going with the furniture. Rearranging. You never knew where things would be when you got home. Katie and Molly and Bridget thought it was funny. Mom's going round the bend, they'd say, but I was scared. They started flinging things at me in the night. Saying I was whimpering and to cut it out.

Then Mom got convinced we had mice in the walls. Just because our cat was staring at the corner of the living room for a long time. She couldn't get into Dad's tool shed, so she took a bread knife and started digging at the plaster. What a mess. There must've been twenty holes in the walls when we got home from school. Looked like a blind person went moose hunting in there.

When Dad got off work, he just said oh for the love of God and called his friend Bill to go for a beer. Mom swept up and put the potatoes on to boil. The rest of them thought it was funny as hell. I went upstairs and sat in the linen cupboard for a long time and I don't even like the dark.

Then Mom started seeing flies in everything. She'd say they were in the breakfast after she made it, and we couldn't find any but she'd fling the whole works in the garbage anyway. We had to go to school with nothing. There was a full carton of eggs once. She cracked them all open to see, and said there were flies in every last one of them. Then she found one in the peanut butter. She said they were in the pillows, and she tore them apart looking, and left the stuffing all over the place. When they got in my hair, she cut it all off short. It was nice and long before. The only pretty thing about me.

Dad decided to go live in the garage. He got someone to help him build a kind of fence wall around it. He put in a bed and some chairs from the living room, and stuck a lock on the door that no one could open even if we could get past the gate in the wall, but we couldn't get the key for that lock either.

He would come over for his meals, such as they were. If Mom was having a bad fly day there'd be nothing at all unless you could distract her and grab a few crackers or a slice of bread. It didn't take long before he got a little hotplate and did his own thing, which was fine for him but not much good to us. The rest of them thought someone should talk to Dad about the situation, but no one would volunteer so they picked me. I didn't want to, but I was so hungry I didn't know what else to do.

I sat out on the front porch one day after school and waited until Dad came home from work, and I followed him to his gate. I told him how Mom was gone nuts and there was never anything to eat when she thought the flies were in it. I said how all the walls were full of holes from her looking for mice and we had no pillows left, and I even said for Christ's sake. He rolled up his newspaper and smacked me with it for taking the name of the Lord in vain. He said what the hell did I expect him to do? He said your mother is insane and so what? Who broke your arms, you can't cook a meal now and then? He said just ignore her. Bar her up in her bedroom. He said he didn't give a damn, he just wanted a bit of peace and quiet because God knows he deserved it.

We tried to get our own meals, but then Mom got thinking that if she went out of the house something would happen to her. After a while there was nothing left in the kitchen to cook even if we could figure out how.

It was Katie decided to call the kids' help line. They must've figured she was joking — she sort of laughs when she gets nervous — because it took three weeks before someone came to the house to check on us. I found out later Joey's teacher called social services, because he was getting to be so dirty and he kept stealing the other kids' recess snacks all the time.

So what happened next was that a woman came to the house and asked could she come in. Mom didn't like the looks of her, I guess, because she told her to go to hell home out of it. But Katie dragged the woman in and showed her the state of the place. The woman made a call and some cops showed up and took us.

The whole while we were packing up our things to take with us Mom wasn't saying anything. Following us around the house and not saying anything. I didn't know what to do. I was scared and I just wanted to hug her but she had her arms all wrapped around herself and I couldn't get in close enough.

When they drove us away she was sitting on the front porch with her fingers all splayed out in front of her face, looking through them like bars on a cage. It was the first time I saw her smiling in I don't know how long.

JOE

I'm up the same time every day to wake the youngsters while Annie gets ready for work – which she hates but what else can she do? Puts in more shifts than anyone else in the world apparently, and her feet killing her. Annie's a nurse. She says she's a nurse. I can't see her getting beyond grade nine, myself, so God knows what she really does for a living. Not that it matters. I'm only too happy to see the back of her heading out. The half hour before the kids leave for school is more tolerable without her.

Brandon has been kept back so many times he should have his own classroom by now. No one knows what to do with him. I suspect that dumb act is a put-on, but he's usually stoned or drunk or both and I've seen the crowd he hangs around with.

Brittney, who changed her name to Raven and won't answer to anything else – if she feels like answering at all – is gaunt and ghastly pale. She used to be pretty but now she's just plain mean looking.

Tiffany is gone to fat and only thirteen. Her mother lets her wear slut clothes – what else you would call them – her belly button hanging out over her tight pants and they falling down around her chubby backside.

Jimmie is six now and still can't talk properly from everyone handing him whatever he points at. He's round as Tiffany and getting rounder. They'll soon be able to roll him to school. Wrap him in a tarp and give a tap with the toe of your boot and there he goes. Might have to if he keeps growing. That or strap him to the roof of the bus – there'll be no seat big enough to hold him. Annie doesn't care what they eat as long as they don't bother her and the cupboards are full of crunchy this and sweetie that – O- shaped sugar with marshmallows.

First off I was cooking nice meals – suppertime anyway – and trying to get the youngsters to eat. I wasn't nagging, but I did encourage. No point in being unhealthy if it could be helped at all. Annie would give me a look to shrivel my soul and ask what the hell anyone who smoked knew about health, she was the nurse around here the kids were fine, just mind your own friggin business for the love of God I'm doing the best I can. If you really want to help with something why don't you try hauling a vacuum around the place once in a while it's like a pigpen and Brandon's room has stuff growing in it for all I know. Jesus! Leave me alone will you? Annie rarely stopped for breath when she went on a rant and I would end up exhausted listening to her.

I do clean the house. The old furniture with oil soap. The worn wooden floors. I dust the ceiling fixtures. Scrub under the big claw-foot tubs in the bathrooms. I like shining things. Keeping them nice. I beat the rugs that Maudie made – hooked – braided – wonderful colours even as they fade and I can still see her fingers when I close my eyes. Working them. Shaping them into ovals and rounds for every room. I keep them clean. Come spring – out to the fence and whack them with a broom. Again in the fall before the snow starts. Maudie always knew when the snow was coming, even after she couldn't see and was sitting in a wheelchair all day, she'd get a sense of it. Bring me out back for a minute, Joe, and sure as hell when she came in again she'd say – snow tomorrow – best beat the rugs today, Joe. And the last time. The last time she said going to be a hard winter this year, Joe, but I'll be sad to miss it all the same. She died a few days later.

Robert was home for the funeral and I could see his heart broke with Maudie's passing. I said he should take her jewellery back with him after. The cameo from her mother and the rings. The sapphire pin I gave her when Robert was born and the silver bracelets she always wore making a sweet sound whenever she moved. I used to say – rings on your fingers and bells on your toes, that's some racket you're making there, Maudie. And I'd have to laugh when she'd dance her arms up close to my face. Like it or lump it she'd say. I'm wearing them 'til I drop.

Robert didn't want them. What am I going to do with them, Dad? It's not like I've got anyone to hand them off to. But he was wrong because it wasn't a year before he met Annie. She was a nurse, he said, though she was working in a restaurant near his apartment for now. She had three children. They weren't seeing each other long when she got pregnant and Robert thought they should go ahead and marry. On the one hand I was proud of my son for doing right by Annie. On the other, I couldn't help but feel she might be taking advantage. I almost said as much when he told me but I knew he'd been lonely long enough.

When Jimmie was three years old, Robert was killed in a car accident. Annie decided to bring his body home to me. All the way from Alberta – with the children. Of course I invited them to stay with me until after the funeral. And then for a few weeks when Annie decided she didn't want to go back out West. Sobbing that she couldn't bear to live there without Robert. Could I help out while she looked for a job? While she saved up for an apartment? While she mourned there wasn't enough money from Robert's insurance to keep her? And I've listened for three years about Robert not providing enough and how would they survive on her income – all five of them – the youngsters wanting something every time she turned around.

Maudie always said I was too kind for my own good. Feeding the dirty old feral cats. The crows and the jays, even the pigeons. Anything that came by looking hungry. She must still be rolling her eyes seeing what I took in when Robert died. Saying Joe. Joe. When does it end, Joe? And I have to admit I don't know.

After Annie leaves I wait until the youngsters have gone before washing up the dishes. Cleaning their mess. I make a pot of good strong coffee and put it in a thermos. Take the lunch I made last night and pack it up to go. Head over to Harry's Groc and Conf to meet my friend. A few weeks ago I stopped there for cigarettes and we got talking. He had just bought the place from Harry Noseworthy who had it for the last fifty years and was wanting to retire to Florida. His name is Halim. The place is not that busy and Halim was sitting outside watching the building across the road being taken apart. After he rang in my smokes he invited me to sit awhile. Brought out another chair and then he asked did I want to join him for lunch. I figured we'd have a bit of pizza or a sub since that's what he sells in the store but he went upstairs to his apartment and brought out two plates of the most delicious food I'd ever eaten. I said maybe we could do it again sometime and I would bring the lunch. He agreed. He enjoyed my company, he said, and thought we could become good friends.

I bought myself a cookbook and tried my own hand at cooking Middle Eastern cuisine. It's not as good as what Halim makes but he says I'm getting there. Annie bitched about the smell. Said it made her gag for the love of God are you trying to poison us? To which I replied that the food was not for her anyway and if she didn't like it she could go open a window and if that didn't work maybe she could find another place to live. That shut her up and I felt bad for the pleasure I took in the look on her face. It was the first time I ever indicated that I might have balls and it scared her good.

Brittney aka Raven started hanging around while I was in the kitchen, which I found unnerving at first, her white face with the half-closed eyes peering out from under the hood of her black shirt, dirty cop boots, jeans with the knees out. I asked her to take her boots off in the house please and she told me to fuck off and left the room but she was back in a few minutes and stood over by the door while I cooked. That night I didn't put all of the food in containers for lunch with Halim. Made up a plate for Raven and set it on the counter. Walked away. She was like the feral cats. If they see you looking they run, never coming beyond the back of the shed. I know to walk slowly, quietly, set the food down and leave. When they feel safe they come out and eat. They might be broken, bleeding, terrified, cold, but they will eat and I think it's not much but it is something, and all I know to do for them. I could feel Maudie smiling when I left the kitchen.

When I returned the plate was empty. After that I cooked every evening – even when it wasn't my turn to bring lunch, and always a serving for the hungry Raven. And she'd eat and clean up after herself, though she never spoke and she never smiled and never came beyond the wall by the kitchen door while I was there. And she still seemed broken, bleeding, terrified, cold, but she ate.

If Brandon hadn't brought home the pup I suppose things might have gone on the same. It was a sad-looking little thing. Had a collar on – spiked leather – weighed more than the dog itself. Fresh cuts and scars on its back and sides. When Brandon put it down on the floor it limped. Growled when I came near it. Backed into a corner and bared its teeth. Nothing that small should be so mean. Annie said get that thing out of here but I gave her a look and she went somewhere else. Brandon said the fellow gave it to him owed him money and he might make a few bucks selling it. Make a good guard dog – so mean and all. Had to wrap it in his jacket so it wouldn't tear his face off. The dog was half-starved and some of the cuts looked infected. Not a male either. Just a sad little girl dog. I asked did she have a name.

Shit-face is what buddy called it. He got a bunch of them from his bitch and this is the only one left. Said it's a pit bull and I could get about 500 for it.

Take that collar off and I'll try to clean her up.

There's no way I want the damn thing now. Just throw it outside. I'll figure some other way to get my money back.

I stepped toward the pup. She growled and snapped and it took some doing but I managed to get the collar off. I put a bowl of milk down by her nose. She lapped at it a minute and fell asleep.

Somewhere along the way Raven showed up. Then she disappeared again. Came back with a towel and the old wicker laundry basket that Maudie used. She made a little nest for the pup and put it in. It yipped once and went right back to sleep. Raven stroked its tiny head. I said I would go to the store and get some ointment for the cuts. Pick up some dog food. Would Raven stay with the pup until I got back? I think she nodded yes but with that hood over her face I couldn't be sure.

When I got home Raven had managed to bathe the pup's cuts. I handed her the ointment and went to start lunch for tomorrow. I put Raven's share on a tray and set it down on the floor near where she sat. She actually looked up at me. In the morning she was still in the kitchen. She had a pillow and blanket and was sleeping near the basket – one hand on the pup. She woke when I came in and jumped up like to run. She had on skinny black pants and an old shirt with holes – the tail end all frayed. Her feet bare. Without the dirty boots and jeans and black hood she looked fragile. She took off and came back a few minutes later in full armour. Gave the pup some food and watched while it ate. Held it close when it was finished.

Annie hollered out that she wasn't going anywhere near that fucking dog and someone bring her coffee right now. Brandon did the honours but not before telling Raven don't get too attached to that thing unless you're planning to pay me for it. Doesn't look nearly as pathetic as it did last night and I might be able to sell it after all.

Raven glowered at him. If you lay a finger on this pup I'll kill you. I swear I'll kill you. She's ours now, isn't she, Joe? She's ours and he can't have her back. Tell him, Joe. So I told him you can't have her back, Brandon. Like hell I can't, old man. Who the fuck is going to stop me? You? He reached for the pup. Kicked at Raven when she wouldn't let go. She turned to the wall. Crouched down. Curled her body around the pup. Ready to take a beating for it. Something in me broke.

I picked up the phone. Said I was going to call the police unless Brandon left the house immediately. You can't throw me out. Yes I can. This is my home and I get to decide who lives here. If your mother wants to leave too that will be fine by me. I'll help you pack. I took Brandon by the arm. He tried to get away from me. Wiry and strong. But I was stronger. Old man was stronger. I dragged him up the stairs.

Annie was watching from the front room. What the fuck are you doing with my son? Let him go! He's leaving, I said. He has to find another place to live. No longer welcome here. In fact, neither are you or your brood. I've had enough. If Raven wants to stay she can.

How the hell am I supposed to afford a place on the money I make? You can't do this.

Yes I can. I was angry. I wanted to hurt her. I had never in my life felt loathing for another being and I was shaking with it. Brandon was squealing let go of me. You're hurting me. I'll have you in jail for this, you old bastard.

Raven came from the kitchen. She held the pup close to her neck. She said she had called the police. Told them there's a fight. They'll be here in a minute. Brandon lunged for his sister. You fucking dyke. You freak. You'll pay for this. No, said Raven. You will. She pulled the hood back from her face to show him the bloody nose and blackening eyes. Smiled at him through swollen lips. You're done now, Brandon. She turned to me. I'd like to call her Lila if that's okay, Joe. I think that's a good name for a puppy.

When the police arrived they were quick to blame Brandon for the damage done and took him away. Annie was livid. She screamed at Raven. What the hell are you doing? You're nothing but trouble, you dirty little bitch. No better than that bastard father of yours. She started to cry. Raven was still smiling. I know, Mom. I know. You mentioned that before. If you want, I can help you pack. I probably should stay home from school today seeing as my face is such a mess. I can call the hopeless shelter for you. I'm sure they can spare a room until you find an apartment. Or another sucker. Up to you.

Raven stood taller than I'd seen her before. Her voice was strong while Annie cried. Behind the blood and black of her there was an odd look. A cold shiver went through me. Beneath the noise – the moaning and weeping – the younger kids yelling what's going on? – I could just make out Maudie's voice. Faint and barely there. Careful, Joe. Careful, my darling Joe.

I have to leave this mess. Leave these people to work out how they will do what I want done. I go to the attic. I haven't been up here since Maudie died. Since I packed her things so carefully to put away. Some in boxes. Some hanging from the rod by the window on the far end. Her dresses.

Coats. I bought special bags for her shoes. Polished each pair and put them away. Her jewellery in its wooden box on the dresser that I always meant to strip and stain. From her mother's house. Someone had spilled paint on it years ago and it needed work. Only after she was buried and gone did I get around to fixing it up. I think I cried the whole time doing it. Cried because she had asked so many times – when are you going to get started on Mom's dresser, Joe? – and I'd say one of these days, Maudie. It was always one of these days, Maudie, and then she was gone and told me not to worry about it anymore. But I did worry about it and after the funeral I spent a week up here – scraping and sanding and finally staining the old thing until it was beautiful – the way she had always wanted it.

Someone has been dusting – not a speck to be seen. Who? Not Annie. She's never cleaned anything that I know of. Not Brandon – that fool boy probably doesn't even know there is an attic. Jimmie? No. Raven? She did have Maudie's laundry basket and I hadn't seen it in years until she made a bed for the pup with it. Did I leave that up here too with all her other things? I always said – Maudie, let's get another one. The wicker was all split and falling apart but she liked it. I said Maudie, do you have any idea how many germs are living in that thing? I bought a new one but she wouldn't use it. Remembered for me how Robert used to nap in it when he was a baby. All snuggled in near Maudie wherever she was in the house.

Maybe Tiffany has been up here. She doesn't say anything. Sits around being fat and eating. But now that I think of it I really don't see much of her. She's rarely around after school. Or the weekends. I assume she's out with friends when I think of her at all. I don't know what to do about this, Maudie. What do I do? But all she says is careful, Joe. Careful.

I am careful, Maudie. I am so full of care I could burst from the pressure. I make my way downstairs. Slowly. Walking older than I am. How did this happen to me? How did these people come to be in my life? Weighing me down. On my chest like the old hag. Squeezing the life out of me.

It's quiet in the living room. In the kitchen there's Raven sitting with the pup. Hood down off her head and I can see the smile on her battered face. And yet there is no pity in me. Just the same chill up my spine as before and my hands shake when I pour coffee. I leave the house without a word. Make my way over to Halim at Harry's Groc and Conf. He is surprised to see me so early. We chat a little about nothing at all and I leave after only a few minutes.

At home I find Raven in the garden. Lying on the grass. Laughing as the pup chews the head off a dandelion. Raven is chatty. The cold is back in my bones and I excuse myself. Go into the house. There are boxes and bags stacked in the hall by the front door. She's been busy. In the attic I sit in the old armchair by the window.

Footsteps on the stairs wake me but I don't move. There's Tiffany. Standing in front of the dresser. She doesn't see me. Opening Maudie's jewellery box she takes out the bracelets. Maudie's bracelets. Puts them on her chubby wrists and smiles as she twirls around – shaking her hands – making the silver jingle the way Maudie did – loving the sound. She looks almost pretty when she smiles. She goes to the armoire. Pulls out a lace shawl that Maudie made. Years it took and it is perfect. Tiffany hauls a chair to the dresser and stands on it to see herself full length in the mirror. Dances with herself in Maudie's bracelets. Maudie's shawl. Humming as she moves – almost graceful. Stretches her arms out as far as they will go and the shawl drapes softly. She is a butterfly.

I move to stand, and frighten her from her perch on the chair. She lands with a thud on the floor. Just a fat child in a mess of lace and silver. A look of terror on her lumpy little face. It's okay, Tiffany. I didn't mean to startle you. Are you hurt? I need to comfort her but I don't think I've spoken more than two words to her since I gave up and left them all alone – but for that Raven who broke my heart with her hunger. And look where that has got me. Poor crumpled thing crawls out of Maudie's finery and is gone.

I go back to the chair by the window and sit. Raven is still in the garden. She freezes suddenly. Looks wildly around for a moment then slowly, calmly raises her head. I think she is looking at me – though how can she see to the third floor – through the tiny window – into my eyes? I can barely make out her features but the darkness that takes over her smile? That I can see. That I can feel. As soon as it begins it ends and she is back to playing with the pup. I can almost hear her laughter. Maudie strokes my face where I've begun to cry.

MICHAEL
AND JESUS

Michael was eighteen years old when he found Jesus. Every Sunday all winter long, through spring and most of the summer while the people already saved were singing and praising and dancing in the glory of the Lord, Michael sat in back and waited until there He was one shiny day – large as life. When the preaching started up again and the topic turned to all of the ugly things that were against the will of God and anyone engaging in such vile activities was damned, Jesus got really uncomfortable and told Michael He was out of there and did Michael want to come too.

On the way back to Michael's house, Jesus said He wouldn't mind going off to live in the woods for a while, so they packed a bag. Change of pants. Warm shirt and jacket. Underwear. Matches. Pocketknife. Toothbrush. Four ham and cheese sandwiches and a pound of good butter. Michael wanted to bring along his hamster but Jesus didn't think that was such a good idea since the woods were full of crows and owls and they might freak the little guy out, which made sense to Michael when he thought about it.

Michael went softly softly to his mother's room to kiss her cheek goodbye and she moved a little in her sleep but didn't wake. He took a small vial of perfume from her dresser to remember her by. Jesus said that Michael should probably write a note to tell his mother that he was fine and might come home someday, but he wasn't sure and he hoped she'd keep thinking about him even when he's not around, love Michael. And Jesus said might as well tape it up in the bathroom because that's the first place she'll go when she wakes up with that headache she got from last night, needing something to put it out with, and Michael said why don't I just leave the note next to her bed with the aspirin and that way she won't have to get up? Jesus said sure if you want to, but I think she'll just go where she always does and not even see them there. It's up to you.

Michael thought more on that and decided Jesus was right, so he stuck the note on the mirror of the medicine cabinet.

It was a long way to the woods and Michael and Jesus had to hitch a ride for part of the trip. A woman in a blue truck stopped and asked how far they were going and Michael said we won't know until we get there and the woman laughed a small laugh and said hop in. Jesus sat in the middle and Michael rode shotgun. The woman with the small laugh talked for a while and then plugged in a CD and they listened to Carrie Underwood who Michael saw once on TV. Jesus and Michael tapped their feet and Jesus sang along to 'Jesus Take the Wheel' but He changed the words to 'Yes, I'll Take the Wheel' and laughed like crazy every time the chorus started.

The woman drove to her very little house in a town that had its feet in the ocean and its head on pillow hills. Michael and Jesus said this place is nice and good. They thanked the woman and started in the direction of the trees. She asked if they'd like a glass of pop or a cup of tea before going. Jesus said He wouldn't mind, but Michael wanted to reach the woods before dark and said no thank you. The woman said well, if you're ever back this way and Michael said he didn't think they would be, but you never can tell.

Walking along Jesus kept singing His 'Take the Wheel' song, until Michael asked Him if He wouldn't mind giving it a rest because He was getting on Michael's nerves and if He didn't stop He might have to find someone else to live with. Jesus sulked for a few minutes but cheered up when one of His chickadees landed on His head and grabbed at His hair. After that He forgot all about the singing, but He kept stopping and saying hello to the birds and a big old rat-kind-of-thing that sat on a log staring at them, and it took almost forever to get to a place that looked like home.

When they did they both knew it at the same time and

they smiled. In a small clearing with birch trees all around was just enough space to sit and have a nice meal and stretch out full length afterwards. They shared one of the ham and cheese sandwiches and Michael wanted to have a nap but Jesus brought up the fact that there was no water to drink that He knew of and maybe they should find some before they got too comfortable. Michael said he was tired after the long trip but he could see the point. So they walked from their clearing in all directions one at a time until they found a blue pond with a shiny stream going into it not five minutes away. They tasted the water to see if it was poison or not and waited on a big rock. When they were still alive a little while later they went back to their new home and had a nap.

Michael could have slept a long time, but Jesus woke him as the sun was setting and wanted to know how they were going to find the water in the dark and wouldn't it be smart if they had a bucket or something so they could bring some back here and not have to wear themselves out every time they wanted a drink. And where were they supposed to use the bathroom? And Jesus was hungry again, wanted another sandwich. Jesus was starting to bug him and Michael wished he'd gone away by himself, though when he thought about it he remembered that going to live in the woods was Jesus's idea in the first place and he probably wouldn't have come up with it on his own.

They ate another sandwich and peed in the woods a little way from the clearing and Michael got upset when he cut his arm on a twig by accident. Jesus told him not to be such a big baby. It's only a scratch, get over it. The air turned cold and they had to put on all of the extra clothes to keep from shivering. Michael curled up small with his back to Jesus and wouldn't talk to Him when he was falling asleep.

In the morning when they went to the pond there were three people fishing. Two young fellas and a short big girl with dirty yellow hair. Michael and Jesus said hello but didn't really mean it because they thought this was their pond now. And the three people didn't seem so happy to see them either. They said they'd been fishing this pond in the summer for years and everyone knows it's their spot. And the rule is when you have a spot nobody else fishes there, same as with berry patches and if they were even thinking about the bakeapples in the bog back of the pond they'd best give that up right now.

Michael was sad but Jesus said what the hell, we can go somewhere else, so they packed up their other two sandwiches and the matches, knife, butter, toothbrush, perfume and started walking back the way they came. The day warmed up and they took off the extra clothes but even so, they were hot, sweaty, needing a shower when they got out of the woods.

Jesus thought it would be a good idea to go see the woman with the small laugh and the blue truck. Michael didn't want to bother her but Jesus remembered that she'd said a glass of pop or a cup of tea, come by if you're ever back this way. They looked for her house and some kids hollered big ugly retard, chased them with a hockey stick. Jesus was all ready to yell back at them dirty little bastards but Michael said it was okay. Jesus said that's pathetic, you should stand up for yourself and He kept looking back and glaring at the youngsters, just daring them to mess with Him, just try it you spawn of Satan.

When they arrived at the house of the woman with the small laugh, they knocked at the door. There was no answer and Jesus said she probably went to work or maybe she's out back. They looked and saw she wasn't, and her blue truck was gone too. Jesus said they should just make themselves at home since she was so friendly, she wouldn't mind if they had some breakfast and got cleaned up and Michael was getting a headache just back of his eyes and he didn't want to argue.

One window was open. Jesus popped the screen and they went inside. The house was so bright and clean. Michael stood up really straight and looked all around for the longest time. The walls were green like baby leaves and the sofa had flowers printed on it – pink and blue like lupines. The floor was shining wood and all of the windows had curtains, wispy and white. There were books on the tables. The rooms ran together with no walls in the way and the sun played on a big plant hanging from the corner of the ceiling.

Michael said he had never seen anything so pretty in all his born days and Jesus laughed. He said it's nice but you know, lots of people live like this. Lots of people have clean houses and money to buy good food and a garden out back to grow a few potatoes and flowers. Not everyone's like you with your whore mother drinking all the time and hauling home ugly men every night and sometimes them going at you if she passes out before they've had enough.

Michael got angry when Jesus called his mom a whore. That's not fair. Why do you want to say something like that about my mother? Well, it's true said Jesus. It's not like you never heard it before so don't be getting all bent out of shape with me. If she didn't have to have you when she did it could have been different but there you were and what choice did she have then?

Michael started to cry. He couldn't call Jesus a big fat liar since his mother already told him that it was all his fault. I do it for you she said, so you can have nice things, though she never did get around to buying him the nice things. When he quit school he found a job sweeping up nights in a place where they made furniture, but one of the older fellows there wanted more hours with his wife expecting and they told Michael not to come back. His mother said good for nothing, don't think you'll be hanging around here living off the fat of the land. I know queers who'll pay to take a run at you, you're on the payroll now and quit your goddamn sniveling. I could have been charging for you all this time, you sneaking around behind my back, giving it away. I know what you've been up to, don't you dare lie to me, and she slapped him hard across his face even though he was almost six feet tall and she was only small.

Michael's head was hurting more and more. Jesus said why don't you lie down on the woman's bed? She won't mind, she said come by any time didn't she? See if she has some medicine you can take and then have a rest.

The woman's bed was clean and Michael took off his clothes so as not to get it dirty and he lay down on top of the soft blue comforter. The window was open and the air coming through was sweet and cool. It ruffled the leaves of a little plant with purple flowers the woman had on the sill and picked up some violet on its way to the bed, covered him all over. In a little while the pain in his head stopped, but another one started where he thought his heart might be. It moved like smoke through his thin body down to his feet and all the way to the tips of his fingers. After a while it didn't so much hurt as warm him, and he slept for a very long time.

JUNIOR
HAPPY COLLINS

The boys are sitting in the lowest branch of the tallest tree in the park.

Missus over there used to have kids. Junior Happy Collins points to a blue three-storey house at the edge of the park. But they got took away and sent off to be orphans. And now they got to scrub floors before the nuns gives them anythin to eat and that's just porridge with no sugar on it. She was forever beating them and that's why they got took away. It happened a long time ago and I never seen them but my Great Nan told me what happened.

What's a nun? asks Ben.

It's sort of a priest but it's more like a woman. And my Great Nan said that they bes real mean to little kids and sometimes they hits them and makes them stand by the sink with their hands in the cold dishwater for days and they're not allowed to go to sleep and when they does they only can lie on the floor and there's a whole crowd of other kids on the floor too and they got to fight over the blanket and it got holes in it.

How come your Great Nan knows all that?

She had the nuns once when she was little and had to go be a orphan herself and she didn't forget. She said she tried but it couldn't go out of her head and that's how come she drinks. That's what she said. She seen a doctor about it once but he couldn't get the nuns out no more than her so he said she should just have a drink. Sometimes they gets real bad when she's lying down and she says, them friggin nuns is at it again, Junior, go to the fridge and get me a beer.

My mom says that drinking is bad for you and she never does it except for a little bit at Christmas dinner.

Your mom prob'ly never had the nuns.

ooo

William was never outside his whole entire life. He lives in that big old house over there. The leafy one with the dirty fence. Them ugly things on top of the posts is called argyles and in the night they comes to life and spits flames at you if you ever dares go near the place. He got no telephone or heat or a stove and fridge and William only ever eats cold beans right out of the can. The roof is full of holes and leaks like nothin else and all the floors got mould on them. The walls is slimy. He got no people left and Great Nan says it's 'cause they're all dead in the basement. Buried in the basement. No, wait, they didn't even get buried. They just got flung down over the stairs when he killed them and that's why the house is so smelly. If you went in you'd die from the stink of it.

How come William doesn't die from it? The stink, asks Ben.

He got used to it. No he never did. I remembers now. He had to buy one of them gas masks like they uses in the wars and he wears it all the time. Even when he sleeps. If he takes it off for one second he'll die.

How did he buy the mask if he never goes out of the house?

He never did buy it. I remembers now. He had it from his grandfather and it was hid in the attic. That's where he got it.

See that mailbox out front? There's killer wasps in that. And spiders. Them poisoned ones from Africa. William never gets mail ever. Sam Mackie is scared to open the box. Once there was a little girl Brownie sellin cookies and she went to William's door and no one ever heard tell of her again. Her mother is all the time out lookin for her but she's gone for good. In the basement with the rest of them I 'spects.

William got a crow and it's really old. Same age as him. No. It ain't even a crow. It's a raven. No. Not even a raven. It's a vulture. I knows 'cause I seen it once and it was eatin a cat.

000

Who's that big kid walking around with a stick? asks Ben.

That's Bobby Frampton. He got somethin wrong with him when he was born and all he can ever do is walk up and down the streets. He don't go to school or nothin 'cause he bes really stunned. They tried to teach him at a special place for retards but it turns out he's too artistic and they made his mother take him back. She works over to the meat market and he just walks up and down up and down until she gets off and then he can go to his house.

How come she can't let him stay home? What if it rains or something?

It don't matter if we gets a tidal wave. He got to stay outdoors. One time she left him home and he burnt down the whole house they was livin in. With a box of matches. And all the people died what was in there. My Great Nan said you could hear them screechin and one old fellow got out by a window up top and broke his head open on the sidewalk. There was blood from hell to breakfast, my Great Nan said. They had about ten people all crammed into that one tiny little house and they all died 'cept for Bobby Frampton and he came out and was pokin at all the dead bodies with his stick. That's the very same stick he still got. There's bits of burnt up skin on the end of it and it can't come off.

Did you just make that up? Now and then Ben is not so sure that Junior Happy Collins is telling the real honest-to-God truth.

No I never. You didn't hear it before 'cause no one ever told you seeing as how you just moved here from away. But you can ask my Great Nan if you don't believe me. Just ask her. She'll tell you. I'm not suppose to go anywhere near Bobby Frampton. He saved some of his matches out of that box he had and if he don't like the looks of you he sets fire to your hair until you burns up and dies.

Bobby Frampton looks up from his patrol and smiles. His mouth is full of very white teeth and his eyes are green and gentle. He is six feet tall – same as the stick he carries. With his free hand he takes a kitten from the pouch of his sweatshirt and holds it out to see. The branch the boys are sitting on is almost level with the kitten's head. Junior Happy Collins pulls back but Ben reaches to stroke it – soft and gray. He can feel it purr all the way through his small boy fingertips.

WANDA

Wanda's father burned down the family home while her mother was at Mass. It was a bright sunny October day. Mild and no wind. The leaves were falling from the big old maples in the backyard. Not gently, Wanda's father noted, while he wandered about, drinking his coffee. Each made a crispy thud as it landed on the grass. He knew it was a matter of mere days before his wife would be after him to start raking. And he would say to her why not wait until they're all down and she would say it looks so messy and if it's either bit breezy they'll be all over the deck too and then tracked into the house and I know damn well that you won't be the one sweeping them up. He sighed. Same thing every year. He might as well get at it before she started in on him.

After Wanda's father burned the house down – which he said he didn't do on purpose but nobody believed him except Wanda – her mother moved in with one of the neighbours.

Mrs. Stoodley was not a tidy homemaker and Wanda's mother was generous with her advice on how to improve that situation. After three days of Wanda's mother showing her where to keep her cookbooks and stack the bathroom tissue and the best place for her odds and ends, Mrs. Stoodley went to Hant's Cove to stay with her own mother for a while. She told Wanda's mother to give her a shout when she decided to move out and spent a week in peace and quiet, playing cards with her mother and drinking sherry. Wanda's mother got lonely and since there was no one else would have her, she took the bus to town and moved in with Wanda – who found her sitting on the front step one day with a box of dishes she had salvaged from the wreckage that had been her home.

Wanda told her mother that she couldn't take her in permanently because she already had three housemates and they were using up all of the bedrooms, but she said she could sleep on a cot in Wanda's room for a few days until she found a place of her own. Wanda's mother had little money. The insurance company was trying to decide if burning down the house was an accident or not. Her pension would pay for an apartment, but nothing else.

She found a small place with kitchen living room dining room all rolled into one. She told Wanda that she couldn't move until she had some furniture and asked Wanda if she would like to bring her stuff and come live with her and Wanda said no. It had taken her thirty years to get away from her mother and there was no way she was going to put her foot in that mess again.

Wanda placed an ad on an Internet site where someone said she could get stuff for her mother. 'I need things for an older lady who is moving into a place where there is no furniture. She has a few dishes but that's all. If anyone can help please call me.'

After three days and no response to her request, Wanda found out from a co-worker that sometimes they have lots of free stuff on the same site where she had advertised and if she wants to come over they can take a look on her computer tonight since Wanda doesn't have one of her own. Wanda didn't want to wait until after the weekend so she could use the computer at work and said sure, why not, and thank you. She made a list of all the things that were free that day to bring home so her mother could pick what she wanted. Her co-worker offered to go with her – she has a truck – and help lug things back to her mother's apartment once she decides what she wants.

Wanda's mother was opposed to the idea of taking other people's cast-offs but not having much money she didn't have a choice.

Wanda's list was long. It included an apple-shaped cookie jar, vases, Grill Pro – whatever that is, said Wanda's mother

– fondue pot, blonde hair extensions, six 1000-piece puzzles of forest scenes not even opened, a hand-knitted bedspread never used 'Mom was afraid the cat's nails might hitch it', a Winnie-the-Pooh blanket and matching pillow sham, treadmill, Skidoo boots, floor-model TV, VHS recorder/player and 72 children's videos, green and pink frog lamp, moving boxes, Cinderella sheets, chesterfield set, pink rug, box spring and mattress, golf shoes, army purse, pool table, glass display case, bunny, three puppies, filing cabinet, bowling ball, dresser, rocking chair, red sunglasses, guitar, crib, computer desk, washer, another washer, wheelchair 'Dad was healed over to the revival', two cement blocks, firewood 'if you can come and take it away yourself', another box spring, Spanish lessons 'if you will help with English', German lessons – same deal, molecular model kit, twenty pounds of frozen meat 'good for dog food maybe', piggy bank, fifty three-ring binders, school bus, half a bag of ferret food and an old wood stove 'suitable for a cabin'.

Wanda's mother studied the list carefully and told Wanda she should pick up the moving boxes first to make it easier. Wanda asked her what else she wanted from the list and Wanda's mother said might as well have all of it but not the puppies or the bunny – Wanda's mother was not one for pets – and not the Spanish or German lessons either since she was never going to need them. Where the hell are you going to put a school bus, asked Wanda and her mother said she didn't know yet but she would think about it.

After he burned down the house, Wanda's father decided to move to Florida where there was no snow to shovel and no leaves to rake that he knew of, and no Wanda's mother. He called an old friend who had moved to the sunshine a few years ago and was all the time asking him to come visit if he ever could. Fred would be happy to have him for as long as he wanted to stay. Wanda's father's clothes were all burned with the house and he said that was fine. Now he wouldn't have to get luggage. He bought a suit and a few shirts and some underwear and stayed over at the Gather Inn until his passport arrived in the mail. He went into town and said goodbye to Wanda who was sad to see him go but happy for him that he was able to get away.

When Wanda and her co-worker took Wanda's mother to see the free school bus, Wanda's mother decided that she didn't really need an apartment after all and could just as easily live in the bus. If it had nice curtains and the seats taken out it would be perfect. Wanda pointed out to her mother that it would never be as clean and tidy as Wanda's mother liked things to be, but Wanda's mother said like hell it won't. Just watch me. Where will you park it asked Wanda, and her mother said I might not have a house any-more but I still have the land it was sitting on. If that bas-tard, meaning Wanda's father, is anywhere near the place I'll just have him flung off it. That's when Wanda told her mother that her father had gone to Florida to live with Fred. I might have bloody well known, said Wanda's mother. That would be just like him. Burning down the friggin house so he could move to Florida. And with that Fred. They'll have their selves killed in a week. Out looking for women every night I bet. Tarred with the same brush the both of them.

The man who was giving away the school bus said that it didn't run very well and asked how far Wanda's mother had to take it. When she told him only about 60 kilometres he said might make it, have either of you ever driven a bus before? To which the answer was no. And then he offered to drive it himself since he was familiar with its quirks and if he didn't get it off his property soon his wife was going to have his balls for bookends because she's got her heart set on building a greenhouse out back where the bus has been sitting for two years. It isn't licensed, he said, but if we go at night there probably won't be too many cops around. And besides it's only a ticket if we do get stopped. I'll have to put some air in those tires first. When do you want to go?

Wanda's mother said as soon as they picked up the rest of the free things on the list. They would bring them all over here and load up the bus. Wanda's co-worker could drive her truck out too and then bring back the man with the free school bus. She had it all figured out. Wanda tried to convince everyone that there was no need for her to go along but her mother said she needed her to help clean up the bus once they got there and her co-worker said there was no way she was spending any time with Wanda's mother alone because she scares the crap out of me, you have to come too. Wanda said she understood.

They spent the rest of the day traipsing around town gathering the free stuff and loading it into Wanda's mother's new home. Wanda's mother decided she wanted to sleep in the school bus that night and the man's wife said, what the hell but you'll have to pee in a bucket. Wanda and her co-worker went out for a few drinks and ended up crashing at the co-worker's place snuggling close in her bed, which Wanda realized was just what she wanted. Her co-worker said it was about time she came to her senses. Wanda said she didn't know she was gay and her co-worker laughed and said well you're the only one who didn't. The next morning they drank coffee and ate muffins and smiled at each other a lot and Wanda's co-worker said she might as well stay with Wanda for the weekend and help clean her mother's bus. Mister could find another way home. They could sleep in the truck, which Wanda thought was an excellent idea.

Wanda's mother was not interested in spending one more minute in town and convinced everyone that they should leave now instead of waiting for the cloak of darkness. The man's wife said the sooner the better, if she had to look at that bus for another minute she'd probably hurt someone. She packed a few sandwiches for the road which they didn't need since the trip would only take an hour and everyone had eaten breakfast including Wanda's mother who had barged in on the man and his wife before the sun came up.

When they arrived in Abel's Arm most of the neighbours came over to help out. They weren't thrilled that Wanda's mother was moving back but nothing much had happened around there since Wanda's father burned down the house and they were bored. Mr. Simms hooked up the free stove – replacing one of the bus windows with a piece of plywood – a hole cut in it to let the smoke out through the pipe he just happened to have in his shed. Mrs. Anstey thought the old bus seats were all right and could use them in the basement for her daughter's friends when they came over – they were noisy and she didn't like having them upstairs in the living room. She took away the ones that Wanda's mother didn't want. Dolly Jones had some oil lamps she wasn't using anymore and offered them for light since there was no electricity and she knew that Wanda's mother liked to read at night.

It didn't take more than a few hours to get things worked out. Wanda's mother decided to have a yard sale in the afternoon and sell the things that she didn't want in her new home. The neighbours thought that was kind of stingy since they had all pitched in to help her but the prices were good and Wanda's mother made $50.38. She kept a box spring and mattress, bed linens, vases, chesterfield, file cabinet, Skidoo boots, golf shoes, pink rug, red sunglasses, bowling ball, cookie jar, firewood and the pool table and made a list of necessities that Wanda could keep an eye out for on the free-things Internet site and anything else that she could sell at her yard sales. She said she would use the pool table to set up on Saturdays and make enough money to buy food, which she can heat on her wood stove, but Wanda should find a barbeque before the weather gets warm again so she can cook outside – preferably a propane one. Wanda's mother likes food that comes out of a can or a box – simply add water – so she only needs a saucepan and she can keep crackers and bread in the cookie jar.

Wanda's father writes to her from Florida once a week and she writes back. Short notes and he is happy to hear from her. He met a very nice woman named Magda. They and Fred go out for dinner now and then. He joined a bowling team. Wanda moved in with her co-worker and they spend a lot of time smiling at each other. They gather up free things on Friday after work and drive to Wanda's mother's place where they spend the night, and sleep in the truck even if it's freezing out.

MILLIE

Millie thinks the only reason the bus stops for her is that she steps out in front of it and flaps her arms. The driver says sure there's no need to be doing that. You're at a bus stop. With twenty other people. I am guaranteed to pull over. And Millie nods and hands him her bus pass. The driver smiles. Millie takes a seat close behind him and watches his face in the rear view mirror while he makes his way through slush and new snow.

At the mall she goes to her bench – same one every time – and takes her knitting out of the carpet bag she found at the Sally Ann that time she was looking for shoes and they didn't have any her size because her feet are so big for a woman. It is a beautiful bag – gold and orange and brown. Faded and the leather handles are worn. It is big enough to carry anything she wants it to hold but all that's in there is her knitting and lunch – a tuna fish sandwich wrapped in wax paper. Sweet milky tea in a thermos bottle.

The mall is nice and warm. Millie folds her coat over the back of the bench. Tucks her gloves in the pockets and her scarf down one sleeve. Her woolen cap down the other. She wipes her eye glasses with the tail of her sweater and watches people for a few minutes before getting to work.

Millie makes socks for orphans. She has never met an orphan that she knows of – other than some children who lived near her in Ben's Cove when she was little. Their dad drowned out fishing and their mother jumped off the cliff the very next day and landed on the rocks all messy and Millie was the one who found her when she went picking mussels. And her mom got mad at her for being out there all by herself – how many times have I told you?

Millie is sure that she will know an orphan when she sees one. He or she will probably have that same look as the children back home before the orphanage came and got them. They were very sad and even though everyone in Ben's Cove took turns having them in and feeding them, they always looked hungry. There used to be a big orphanage in the city but they took it down and now there are only houses and stores instead. Millie doesn't know where all the orphans live now and she doesn't know who to ask. Still, they have to be somewhere and Millie knits on. She'll be ready when one turns up.

Millie doesn't knit quickly but she knits well. Each sock is made of many colours. All stripy and bright. No two are ever the same so one sock will not resemble its mate, unless you count size and beauty. Sometimes a person will come and sit next to Millie as she knits. Ask if she sells her beautiful socks anywhere. Millie says no. She's waiting for orphans. Once a young woman, who looked hungry, sat down and watched her for the longest time. Millie decided to give her a pair but when the young woman realized the socks didn't match she said thank you no. Millie found that strange after all the going on about how beautiful they were. But never mind. More for the orphans.

When Millie has finished her knitting for the day, she packs up her carpet bag and carries it – along with her outside clothes – to another bench on the second floor of the mall where she drinks her tea and eats her sandwich. After lunch she wanders about looking in shop windows at the lovely things. At two o'clock, she goes to the bench across from the wicker store to read. If some people are already sitting there she goes to the pet shop and watches the fish and bunny rabbits until they leave.

Millie started reading many years ago when the department store she worked in, cleaning up at night, closed down for good. She got a card for the library and goes there every other Saturday. It is just as warm in the winter as the mall is. The woman at the desk asked what kind of books she was interested in and Millie couldn't say really since the only one she remembered was The Mill on the Floss in school and that was boring as dirt. She started with the A's in fiction. She's at C now and Barbara Cartland who seems to have written a hell of a lot – too much if you were to ask Millie's opinion – she must be at it day and night. Millie gives a book twenty pages. If she doesn't love it by then, back it goes to the library, which doesn't mean she gives up on an author just because the book is no good. Millie figures even writers must have bad days.

Come five o'clock, Millie is ready to go home. Back in her room – bathroom down the hall – across the street from, and one floor higher than, the Chinese restaurant named Lo Wing, Millie puts today's socks in the cedar trunk that also serves as coffee table. Goes to the stove to boil water for tea. Jack will come by later. They like to sit in the window with the lights off and watch the people who eat at the Chinese restaurant. Neither of them has ever had Chinese food and Jack says it's because it has too many things in it. Jack doesn't like for different foods to touch, which is why he never eats vegetable soup.

Millie says that wouldn't matter to her and she would like to have a little taste one of these days. She thinks it might be expensive though.

The people who eat at the restaurant are the same ones over and over. There is a woman who comes in every evening and puts her coat on the chair across from her. Jack says she's afraid someone will try to sit there. Millie thinks it's because she is lonely and pretends she has a friend to eat her dinner with. She can see the woman's mouth move, and not just from chewing. More like talking to someone who isn't there. Before she leaves, the waiter helps her on with her coat and she smiles at him.

There's a young man who rides a bike – even in the winter – who goes once a week on Monday. He always reads a book while he eats. And when he finishes a page he tears it out. Millie thinks he's rich to be doing that and also foolish. Wasteful.

Jack said once that if Millie really wants to try Chinese food he could get her some. He said that lots of times when people's eyes are bigger than their bellies the waiter puts their leftovers in little boxes and they take them home. He said that one of these days he could follow someone like that and snatch the boxes out of his hands and hide around back until he's gone. Then he'd come up to Millie's room and she could have her taste. It might even still be warm.

Millie laughed at Jack for that. Told him she doesn't want other people's leftover dinner. And besides what if Jack got caught? He's not allowed to do anything wrong ever again since the time he had to go to jail for eight years about what happened at the boarding house over on Caines Street.

And Jack said that yes, he supposed it was a bad idea. He doesn't want to go back to that place. And Millie said good because she would have to miss him all over again if he did.

In a little while, Millie asks Jack if he would like some dinner and he says yes. She puts on an apron covered with embroidered birds and flowers that someone made special but ended up at the Sally Ann. She opens a can of tomato sauce and a box of dried pasta. Puts each in pots to cook. Jack eats his noodles with butter and salt. Millie likes to mix hers up with sauce and sprinkle on a little cheese. For dessert, Jack goes down to the corner store for apples. Green for Millie and red for himself. They drink tea until it's time for bed. Millie kisses Jack on the cheek – the one with the long purple scar – and he goes back to his room down the dark hall.

MICE

The first one is in a kitchen cupboard. A wee face and two paws in a gap between ceiling and wall. Squeaking. Whiskers quivering. Stuck. I stare and it stops shaking. I reach in close and push up on the ceiling and it disappears. Thank you, ma'am, and gone. Might have been nice if you could stay and chat awhile, mousie.

I go up the stairs to the bathroom. Look in the mirror to check. Make sure I am still here. When I decided to paint the kitchen I took the little mirror down that was hung on the far wall by the back door. Since then I can find no evidence of self unless I run upstairs to the bathroom to check. I do it several times a day whenever I am feeling a little gone. You would think that a glance at my hands or feet might be enough but you would be wrong. It's the face that tells all. The eyes. Anybody in there? Anybody? Yes. There I am. Hello me. I see you haven't left yet. Hello.

There are three more next day and I scoop them up in a dustpan. Put them outside in the cold ocean wind to fend for themselves. They are back later that evening – I recognize the grin on the small one. Well. I guess you'll be staying then.

I have cats. Some youngster came by with a couple one day. Kittens. Hungry and squalling for a mother. I was down to the dump, missus, and I found them in a old cardboard box. Mom won't let me keep 'em and they'll just die if I puts 'em back. There's rats would eat 'em for sure.

Like hell I said to myself. Your mother told you to get rid of the last batch your ugly pet had and you're too lazy to do it.

There's fellows goes there to shoot at the gulls and they would kill cats too. Well – what is it, punk? Rats or fellows with guns? Never mind, I said. I'll keep them but don't bring any more. But he did. Next day. These were in worse shape than the first two. A day hungrier. A day colder. Starving, so I shoveled warm milk into their tiny mouths until they shut up and went to sleep.

The mother cat came hanging around so I let her in. She tried to nurse them but she was pathetic, and dried up in the bargain. I gave her a can of tuna fish and wished her luck. Here's a basket and a blanket. Snuggle down the lot of you and try not to get in my way. I'm painting.

The old woman next door comes by while I am up to my ears in puce. That's a nice colour you got there, she says. I likes purple. It's puce, I tell her. Puce. She is as round as she is tall which is not to tell much. She doesn't come to my chin. She has the same red – carrot – hair as all the others in that house, but graying. She could be 45. She could be 100. The neighbours on the other side say that her husband – who hasn't been seen in years – sleeps on the daybed in the kitchen and drinks. They say he fathered all of his grandchildren as well as one great grand. I don't know. That's what they say.

She brings seal flipper pie and even if I want to eat it, I cannot. The grime in the plate's patterned rim puts me off. I tell her thanks. I'll have that for my dinner later on. No sense hurting her feelings. I flush it away when she leaves.

Walking through the meadow above the ocean I come across her. Sitting near an ancient root cellar. Rocking back and forth with her apron pressed to her face. Wiping tears. Her eyes are black and her old arms bruised below her dress sleeves. He's after having his way with me. Who? My son. He's home from Ontario and he's after having his way with me. Your son did this to you? Yes. He's all the time at me when Ruby's not here. Ruby is her dead son's wife. She went into town when she heard he's back. I don't know what to do. I tell her she can come to my house and clean up a little and maybe we can call someone. Who can we call? I can't be letting people know about this. Well if you can tell me you can tell the police. No I couldn't tell the police. I couldn't do that. I'll just stay here until he's gone down to the club. If you wants to bring me a drink of water that would be all right.

I head in to town for a few days to visit a friend. Can you see me? Am I still here? Oh you silly. What are you talking about? Let's go out and drink our faces off – have a bite to eat.

When I come home to the cove the smell hits me hard across the face. I follow it to the linen closet, and among the blankets, baby blankets, some poor mouse has had a litter. They have died and rotted quickly and I open windows to air the house. The baby blankets. They died in the baby blankets. There is no baby. And I wonder what kind of joke is this? Dead mice in the baby blankets and there is no baby.

Mice make tiny footprints in the cupboards. (How can you tell there's been an elephant in your fridge…?) They tear open cat food bags. They are partial to Melba toast and Brie. They party in the back of the sofa. They invite friends. I tell them no smoking and stay out of the vodka. The cats are useless. They climb curtains. They eat. They sleep. They do not mouse.

The day I bought this house I ran happy beyond the back fence to the ocean. I did not see the gulch until I was almost over its edge. Straight down a hundred feet I might have been but for good treads on the sneakers. Down with the old cars and chairs and who knows how many dead dogs. There wasn't always a dump here and even still, it's far to go when you can just shove things over to sink.

At night I sit in the black of the living room window and stare. I can see my reflection in the glass. Hello. Are you? Are you here? I see you but tell me anyway. Speak. There are two mice on the floor beside the bookcase arguing over a potato chip. It's mine. Smack. No, it's mine. Give it to me. Smack. Will you two cut it out? All I ask is a minute's peace at the end of the day, but no. You've got to be squabbling. And I stamp my foot on the floor. They look up for a second but go right back at it. I run upstairs to the bathroom to check in the mirror. Yes. I'm still here.

APRIL

April left the children for a minute to pick up a few bottles of water at the convenience store. That's when the SUV came around the corner and slammed into her car. The driver was eighty-five and half blind, but the reason he lost control was a heart attack.

The old fellow's foot was resting on the brake but not hard enough to stop the car – and the scene played itself in slow motion. The SUV crawled down the hill with April's car in front – through traffic lights – sideswiping three other vehicles – finally ramming into a low stone wall where it stopped.

April ran – kicking off her shoes as she went. Later, a pretty girl with dangling earrings and a hula hoop found one of them and kept her jewellery in it for years after.

When she reached her car the people who had scattered out of harm's way were gathering close and no fewer than sixteen of them had called 911. The children were screaming, except for the baby, though she was looking wild-eyed. There were a few cuts but little else to see at first glance. Talk of miracles broke out even before the ambulance arrived.

At the hospital, having been assured that the children and the baby were fine – unbelievably fine – it pays to own an expensive car – nothing to worry about – we'll keep them in overnight anyway – she relaxed.

○○○

Jane Hollis cleaned her hands and put away her latest canvas, a painting of dark trees with a blue moon shouting through their twitchy branches. She poured herself a glass of scotch – neat – and sat to read, at last, the letter that had arrived several days earlier from her youngest child.

Dear Mom,

Bob will probably show up at your door in a month or so –
looking for me. He'll be all worried and down in the mouth – I
don't understand, Jane, why would April leave me? Why would
she take my children from me? Why? Here's where you ask him
what the children's middle names are and if he gets that right, ask
when they were born.

I know what you're thinking, Mom. It isn't that bad – for the
sake of the children – life is not a bed of roses – you called the tune
now pay the piper – what about the poor little things growing up
without a father?

Well Mom, it's like this. We haven't heard tell of him for over
two weeks now. That's the last time he called from his 'hotel' in
New York. After he hung up I realized that I'd forgotten to ask
him something about the furnace – it was cutting in all the time
and it's been so warm out – July for goodness sake – so I hit *69
and got the number. The phone rang and – wait for it – a woman
answered. I figured she was new on the desk since she didn't an-
nounce the name of 'hotel whateveritis' when she picked up. I
asked to be put through to his room – she was a little fluttery but
there he was right by her side I expect, since nothing rang before
he answered. He was cool. Reminded me that I was never to call
while he was away on business unless it was an emergency. Business, I said. What kind of business are you up to, Bob? Monkey
business? I can't believe I said that! Monkey business! It is so not
like me but when I hung up – actually he hung up – I realized it is
exactly like me. I ran to the hall mirror and there I was. The kind
of person who says monkey business. My hair was fluffy. My
make-up was fluffy. Perfect and fluffy as if I'd gone to Fluffy University and my pink blouse was fluffy and my necklace and my
earrings, so I called Poppy to come over quick I need help. And
even though I hadn't seen her for two years – not since the time
she shook me hard to rattle my teeth and slapped me and stomped
out of my house – my fluffy house, Mom – she came over.

I prepared lunch for the children and waited for Poppy. And when she got here I said – look at me – just look at me, Poppy. Have you ever seen anything as pathetic in your life and she said not for a couple of years, now, why do you ask? I said how did I get to be so pink and fluffy and she said we all saw it coming. We warned you but you were so determined.

I told her about saying monkey business and she didn't get my point – lots of people say monkey business – but when she thought about it she realized that in combination with the rest of my make-up it could be a bit of a straw – you know – to-break-a-back straw?

I asked why on earth anyone would want to live like this and she said hell knows but that you all have your theories.

Have you noticed how clean my children are? Have you? I asked and she said yes, it is rather sad and then she said the family started a therapy fund a few years back but you all realized that Bob probably has the best insurance in the world so instead you went and bought some goats and chickens for people in places where they don't have enough goats and chickens. She said the name but I can't remember. I think there was a water buffalo involved as well. I told her that was an odd thing to do and she said not really, do they even own a paint brush, and I thought she was talking about the goat and chicken people still but she meant the children. My children.

And then I said this house – who would want to live in a house like this? And she said no one that she knows and where did I get my decorating skills. I said I don't have any but I found pictures in a magazine and called someone to come and do it. And find the same furniture and paint the walls the same and there it is. I think it was Martha Stewart.

And she said you had Martha Stewart decorate your house? And I said no – it was a Martha Stewart magazine. And she said she doubted that because even Martha's places look lived in and mine looks like a Toronto condo.

Then Paulie came in and wanted another sandwich so I went to make one for him. And Poppy said there's another thing. That boy is thirteen years old and you're making his sandwich? And calling him Paulie? His name is Paul. Say it. Paul. And it sounded strange on my tongue but I did and have tried to remember to call him Paul ever since. And I told him it's okay to prepare his own lunches even though he makes a terrible mess with crumbs in the butter and all, and doesn't clean the counter properly.

Poppy said to stop using so much antibacterial crap – she called it crap – or the kids wouldn't have a decent immune system between them. Among them? Whatever.

Then she asked if she could take Sue-Sue – Suzanne Suzanne Suzanne – shopping since she looks like a Barbie doll and it's time she picked out her own friggin clothes – Poppy's word, not mine – and my darling came back all black and ragged and Poppy was pleased as punch – scratch that – delighted – that Suzanne is heading in the 'Goth' direction.

I can still call the baby Bekki since she's only eight but next year she'll be Rebecca. I have to stop referring to her as the baby. So many rules and I was having a hard time following so Poppy took to coming over every day and reminding me. She said I had to go along with her if I want her help. No questions asked.

After I shaved my head it got easier though the children don't want to be seen with me until it grows in. That was my very own idea and you should have seen the look on Poppy's face when she saw me. Ha! But I had to do it. Starting over. It seemed right and I love it. I wonder what colour it will be.

Poppy said to get rid of the furniture and I should have a yard sale but if I did that the neighbours would know something was up so I had the whole works put in storage. The house is pretty naked now and I can't have any more furniture until I find things I like and since I don't know what I like yet it could be some time. There's an echo.

Suzanne has plastered her room with posters of vampires. She wanted to paint the walls black but even Poppy said that was taking it too far so she settled for red and she wants to do it herself. Poppy promised she'd get her the brushes and whatever else she needs. I've never painted anything in my life so I wouldn't be much help to her.

Paul has found a friend on the street and he goes swimming at the park. Without me. And he says it's much nicer than going to the club pool. The other night he stayed out until after dark. I was frantic but Poppy says I have to give them some rope or they'll hate me later. I don't understand her reasoning. You gave us more freedom than any of our friends had. I don't know about the others but I don't see what good it did me. No one else I knew was allowed out as late as I was and I spent a lot of time wandering around by myself. You seemed to think that I should be taking advantage of my good fortune so I couldn't very well come home early and hurt your feelings. Poppy didn't want anything to do with me and neither did Arthur or Frank, being so much older. I was terribly lonely and sad. I think that might be how people feel when all their friends up and die before they do.

Anyway – that's neither here nor there. Fact is – Bob called and said he won't be back for another month – some big deal that needs more work – but I expect he's punishing me for calling him at his 'hotel'. He didn't even ask about the kids. He transferred a month's worth of grocery money into my account so we'd have enough to eat – big of him – and that was that.

I took all of my clothes to a consignment place – that's where they sell them and give you the money later and when I checked the woman told me they're almost all gone. Poppy said someone in town must be having a Mad Men theme party. She can't figure another reason why anyone would want my dresses. I don't know what she's talking about but I should be getting the money for them soon. Of course then I was down to practically nothing and Poppy took me to some thrift stores. You would be amazed, Mom. The prices are ridiculous. Poppy picked out some things for me to try on and it turns out I am a blue jeans kind of girl. Ha. Who knew?

I put my jewellery in a safe deposit box. Not in our bank either. I opened an account at a different one. Poppy said to – just in case. In case what? I asked her, and she said, in case Bob decides to take revenge and you end up a pauper. That put me off. It never did occur to me how Bob might react to what I've been doing. I have to say I was a little down about that. I had in the back of my mind to pack up and leave – not that there's much left to pack – ha. Find a new place to live with the children. Get a job. I had one in high school, remember? And I do have that degree. About time I put it to use. Or I could go back to university and update my skills. What skills, you might ask. Good question. I guess I'll find out.

When I told the children what I planned to do – moving and all – they were a little upset. Well. A lot upset. I said they would have to go to public school now and probably drop out of the usual extracurricular activities. All of a sudden Suzanne remembered a whole bunch of friends I've never heard tell of before and Paul was going to join the debate team and play hockey for his school and join the newsletter committee. This is the boy who's never even put on a pair of skates before. And he couldn't argue his way out of a paper bag if his life depended on it.

I don't think Bekki actually cares what she does as long as she can wear her fairy-princess wings. I offered to get new ones since they are looking so ratty but Bob bought them for her last year sometime and all of a sudden she's attached to them. Or them to her if you get my drift. Ha. She dug them out of her closet and hasn't taken them off for two weeks. If she didn't insist on wearing them to bed they might last a little longer but there's no convincing her of that. I tried to take them off her so I could wash them but she screamed blue murder.

I wish you'd get a phone, Mom. I've been writing this letter for two days now and it would be so much easier just to talk to you. But I suppose then we would get into an argument about something. Poppy, most likely. I know you don't have much time for her but she's really been a wonderful support to me. If it weren't for her I'd still be fluffy and pink. She is showing me how to rid myself of the trappings that aren't really me. To express myself clearly. Did I mention that she signed me up for a series of classes on how to get more in touch with the true me? All about angels and chakras and crystals and whatnot. A friend of hers presents them. Brings in experts from all over. She says it will do me the world of good. She gave me a bunch of books to read too. Starting with The Celestine Prophecy. Can't wait to get started.

So. That's it for now. I'm off to get Poppy and then we're going to Middle Cove with the children to look for whales. I just wanted to give you a heads up about the situation. As soon as we move I'll send our new address but only if you promise not to give it to Bob.

Love you,
April

o o o

From the hospital, April called Poppy to let her know what had happened and please bring some shoes since she had kicked hers away in her haste. She hadn't been off the phone for ten minutes when her sister showed up with a bag of aloe leaves and a bunch of sage. The former to anoint the children's wounds. The latter to rid their room of any negative thoughts that previous patients might have harboured while undergoing treatment in the same beds. You can never be too careful. The fight that ensued between Poppy and the staff when she set the sage afire and started chanting was hushed but serious. One of the nurses confiscated her weeds and had security escort her off the premises.

On the sidewalk, April caught up with Poppy who had lit a joint and was daring anyone who passed to go right ahead and do something about it. Nobody seemed to care. April told her that the children had to stay in for observation. Poppy said well we should go to Harper's house and keep vigil. She'd call her friends and set up a prayer group. April said that she felt the doctors were doing a good job with the children and besides, their injuries didn't appear to be serious to which Poppy responded that the medical profession consisted of a bunch of charlatans who didn't know their asses from their elbows and couldn't be trusted to take care of a houseplant, let alone precious human life. April conceded Poppy was probably right about that and went inside to say goodbye and she'd be back in the morning to take them home. Neither Suzanne nor Paul seemed fazed by the ordeal, though Bekki was weepy about the nurses taking her wings, saying they were too filthy to be allowed in a hospital room and should be burned. April said she would have them cleaned so Bekki could wear them tomorrow when she got out.

The car had been towed from the scene of the accident by the time April and Poppy returned. Poppy thought they'd best get the prayer group rounded up before dealing with anything else and the insurance company could be called later. April's purse was still in the car along with the children's health cards that should be brought to the hospital immediately but no matter, Poppy said. First things first.

Admissions had different priorities and when April didn't return with the necessary information and since Bob's name was also on the children's medical records, along with his cell phone number, he was called. Before Poppy and

April had made their way to Harper's apartment – over the tattoo parlour on Caines Street – he was in a cab to the airport. By the time they had lit their sandalwood-scented candles and formed a circle on the floor he had pissed off everyone at the American Airlines desk in New York and was seated on the next flight to Toronto where – if they knew what was good for them – the fools at Air Canada would have him booked to go home. Whatever Bob is, he loves his children, and if their middle names and birthdates aren't on the tip of his tongue so what?

Praying at Harper's place was a long drawn-out affair. Harper has written the names of all the major world religions – as well as some of the lesser known ones – on little pieces of paper that she keeps in a blue ceramic bowl. The bowl sits in the centre of her altar surrounded by statues of Mary and Jesus, the Buddha, various Hindu deities, a picture of Baha'u'llah, and representatives of Islam, Judaism, Native North American and the rest as well as bits and pieces from Wicca and Voodoo. Harper is a spiritual slut. From the blue ceramic bowl, each of the women gathered took, in turn, a piece of paper and read out the name of the religion she had picked. Harper looked up a suitable prayer, in this case, healing of children crushed by an SUV or something close enough, and the women prayed. There was plenty of chanting and weeping and twice the man who ran the tattoo parlour downstairs came knocking to see if everything was all right.

At first April was embarrassed to be part of the gathering but Poppy assured her that if she could only let go her rich white attitude she would be fine. She did her best to relax and maybe she did or maybe the smoke from the cheap candles – of which there were many – sucked the air out of the room. Either way she fell asleep half-way through the ceremony and no one had the heart to wake her.

When the women had prayed themselves hoarse they drank a few bottles of Harper's homemade wine and left. Covered the sleeping April with a black shawl and let her be. She woke to find Harper sprinkling her with holy water that she steals from the Basilica on Sundays. The children will be fine said Harper and April said she knew that already. The doctors had told her as much yesterday. Harper said, what the hell was all that about last night then? Poppy said they were in bad shape and might not live. Shit I hate it when she does that. I had better things to do than spend half the friggin night praying when there was no need. Some of us had planned to go do yoga at the beach – full moon and all. Shit. That's the last time I do anything for her. She's getting to be a real pain in the ass.

That's my sister you're talking about, said April. Yeah, yeah, whatever, said Harper. She's still a pain. Are you almost ready to leave? I have a dental appointment to get to.

Out on the sidewalk, April, with no purse, no keys, not even a quarter to make a call, wondered what she was supposed to do next. Walking, she realized that Bekki's fairy wings, the ones she was going to have cleaned and ready to fly, were still in Harper's apartment. She went into a second-hand bookstore and begged to use their telephone. Poppy answered but told her that she should take this opportunity to discover her true strength. There are thousands of people in worse situations and somehow they manage to survive and besides she had a lunch date with a really nice man she'd been wanting to get together with for ages. April got angry. Poppy said something about getting back to the moment and hung up.

The man behind the counter of the bookstore gave April directions to the hospital. It was a long walk and uphill half the way but within an hour April was there, having got lost only once. She was hot and sticky and her feet hurt from wearing Poppy's too-big shoes. Blisters on her heels. In the room where the children had been there was no sign of life. She flagged down a nurse to find out what had happened and was told that their father had taken them home an hour ago – about the same time that you said you'd be here and the little one was very upset about not having her fairy wings, you know. You really shouldn't make promises to children that you have no intention of keeping. Their father seems like a very nice man.

April told the nurse to go fuck herself. At the main desk she was informed that she couldn't use the phone because it was for emergencies only but there was one in the lobby. April still had no quarters and asking didn't get her very far. People wouldn't even look her in the eye and no wonder. She was a sight, all grubby and wrinkled from sleeping on Harper's floor – stinking of sandalwood–scented smoke. Her shaved head didn't help and there was blood on her shirt from hugging the children yesterday. If she'd had the energy she would have cried.

April set out to walk the two miles from the hospital to home. In a small park she sat on a boulder near a bed of flowers and finally shed a few tears. They streaked her face with the last of yesterday's mascara and her nose was red and running when she climbed the stone steps to her front door.

Bob took one look at his bedraggled wife and scooped her up in his arms. Carried her to their bed where he gently removed her dirty clothes and tucked her in. Kissed her forehead and closed the door to let her sleep. Told the children not a peep out of you until your mother wakes, okay? A knock on the door brings a telegram from the only person he knows who still sends telegrams.

April. What the hell are you thinking, listening to your sister? Poppy is out of her mind and you know it. I'll be arriving tomorrow morning. Your mother.

When Bob met April, she was disguised as a free spirit. Beautiful and strong. Her hair moved when she did. Her legs could take her wherever she wanted to go. Her arms were long and lean. In bed she was soft and warm. She was working on a Master's thesis in Geology and could make the meanest rocks sound sexy. They were introduced at a party given by one of Bob's old friends. It was the closest thing to love at first sight that any of the other guests had seen. They still talk about it now and then. Remember when? It was good.

Bob finished his PhD in Marine Technology and asked April to marry him please. April packed her papers away and quit her work though this was not what Bob had intended at all but she seemed so eager to become a stay-home wife that he didn't say anything other than are you sure, sweetheart?

Within a year of marriage April had a baby and Bob might as well have shot himself for all the good he was. He tried to worm his way into the duo that was April and Paul, but she kept him out. The circle grew with Suzanne and Rebecca, but still excluded Bob. She talked about the children when she talked to him at all. Her life was completely taken with them. She became a smother and nothing Bob could do made a difference. Let me change the baby. Let me take them to the park. Let me cook supper. I'll make their lunches. I'll drive them to school. For once will you let me pick out a birthday gift? Let me read to them tonight. April held tighter with each advance Bob made. He gave up. Not to say he didn't love April more than anything in the world but she needed him like she needed a hole in the head. He began taking longer trips than necessary. Speaking engagements all over the world. Sometimes he simply went on vacations to Japan or Australia. Once he went camping and climbed a mountain. When he finally accepted that he would never be more than sperm donor and breadwinner he tried having affairs. That didn't work out too well so he found a lady of the night who was put off by his lack of interest in the usual until she realized he was going to pay her anyway. He read to her – poetry and some of the books he thought his children might have liked had he been permitted to spend tuck-in time with them.

April slept through the night and on into the next day. Bob took a spare room so as not to disturb her. When he woke he looked in on his dirty wife and then prepared breakfast for the children. He called around and asked a lot of questions until he found a Boys and Girls club. Spoke to the person in charge and, ignoring his children's protests, drove them to a nearby park where fifty other kids were playing softball or swimming or making crafty things. Keep an eye on each other and I'll be back to get you by 5, he said. Have a good time and listen to the counsellors. To the woman who looked the most frazzled, he handed two hundred dollars. Why don't you order pizza for the children at lunchtime and the most frazzled woman almost cried with gratitude since her heart broke every day when she saw what some of these mostly poor youngsters had brought to eat, or not. She calculated quickly and asked Bob if she might buy a few fruit and vegetable trays as well and he said whatever you want. His children, when he glanced at them from the car, looked pathetic, and if they all stuck their thumbs in their mouths right now could be mistaken for morons. His heart broke a little.

At home he took a long look at what was no longer there. He re-read his mother-in-law's telegram and called

Poppy. Left a message telling her to get in touch immediately or he'd hunt her down. She responded within two minutes. He smiled to himself when he heard her voice. Where the hell is my furniture? And Poppy tried to sound as vicious as he did but failed. It's in storage, and she told him where, but I have the key. Bring it over now. I suppose you want her jewellery too, then? Bob hadn't noticed it was missing. Yes. It's at the TD Bank. I have the key to the deposit box. Get your ass over here, said Bob and he sounded that angry she took a cab.

Bob walked upstairs to check on April, who was still asleep. Making soft little snore sounds. He went to the garage and hauled out an old blue armchair and placed it in the living room near the fireplace that had never been lit, and sat, his long legs stretched way out in front and his hands linked across his flat belly. He put his head back. Closed his eyes and waited.

When Poppy came into the house he was still sitting but opened his eyes. Just give me the keys and leave please. She placed the keys on the mantle and left. Bob smiled. He was still smiling when Jane arrived in a whirl of black cape and grey curls. Carpet bag stuffed to overflowing. Where is April?

Looking at her bald-headed daughter, Jane began to laugh loud enough to wake her, who sat up and raised her arms for hugs. Jane obliged, rocking the now-weeping April back and forth as Bob ran a bath. Jane sat on the vanity while Bob washed his wife's lovely body – her fuzzy head – with warm soapy water. Once she was clean and rinsed and dry and wrapped in a towel they all went back to the bed and sat while April talked. And talked.

When she finally wound down, Bob said he had to run some errands if Jane would be so kind as to stay with April. He'd pick up the children later on and bring home supper. No need to cook anything. Good, said Jane, I gave that up a few years ago. Where are the children anyway? They're having fun, said Bob. I hope. That would be a nice change, said Jane. Do they even know how? We'll find out, said Bob and left.

At the storage facility, Bob arranged for a truck to take everything to the Salvation Army Thrift Store. He took April's jewellery from the bank to a reputable bauble shop and told the diamond expert to get rid of the stuff for him. He called a local animal shelter and asked if he might see some of the dogs they needed fostered because his children had never had a pet other than a few goldfish that were quite useless and not a lot of fun. The woman who answered said come on over please. Last week we brought in a litter of pups from some fool who left them outside in a crate in the heat with no food or water for a few days and almost killed the lot of them. They're Shepherd Lab mixes and judging from the size of the paws on them they'll be huge when they grow. Perfect, said Bob. There's no point having a dog if it isn't big. When he saw them he couldn't decide which one and it took some time to convince the woman that he would provide an amazing home for all four. He had to supply references and wait while they were called. He had to sign papers promising this and that. He had to purchase everything the woman thought he needed starting off before she would let him take them home and even then he was on probation and she'd come around in a few days to see how it was going. He gave her a sizable donation before leaving. She said, that won't get you off probation but thank you very much all the same.

When he brought the puppies home, Jane was all over them. They were the cutest things she had ever seen. April was shocked. The first thing they did was pee on the off-white Berber carpet. Well, said Bob, I guess that will have to go too. Back to hardwood. But Bob, said April. Hardwood? It's so cold underfoot in the winter. We do have central heating, said Bob, and fireplaces. But Bob, said April, you know how dirty things get when you have a fire. Bits of bark from the logs. Ashes all over the carpet. No carpet, said Bob. Hardwood. Easy to clean. Oh, said April. Yes. Hardwood.

Bob went to get the children from the park. Rebecca was crying and raced to him to sob in his arms. Her nose was burnt and freckled and runny. She had picked out a friend from the crowd and someone else took her and it wasn't fair. Sob. Sob. I'm never coming back here again in my whole entire life, Daddy. Yeah, said Bob, you are. Day after tomorrow. Paul came running from another direction. Do we have to go right now? Some of the boys are just getting a game on the go. Soccer. Not today Paul. But you can come back tomorrow if you want. Suzanne had learned to make yarn flowers. Ms Edwards's sister is getting married in two weeks and we're making decorations for her wedding. I'm going to do some black ones for my bedroom. It's real easy.

At home the children went wild – tired as they were from their most unusual day – to see puppies and their grandmother. April tried to get them to take showers – she had never seen them dirty – but no one wanted to and Bob said as long as they wash their hands before dinner they'll be fine. He told them to take the puppies outside and make sure the gate is closed so they don't run out to the street. He gave them plastic bags to pick up any poop that might happen. Oh dear, said April. Poop.

Bob went to his armchair – removed the afghan that April had already placed there – and sat to make a few phone calls. He cancelled his next two speaking engagements. He went online to look up carpet removers and arranged to have a few fellows over next morning. He called a friend and asked who made his furniture and how to get in touch. His friend asked if April had died or what, and Bob smiled. Only one of her he said. And smiled again.

April woke next morning to sounds she never thought she'd hear in a home of her own. Squealing children. Running children. Barking puppies. And one that she hadn't heard for so long, it took a full minute to recognize. Bob's laughter. She dressed and made her careful way down over the stairs to the living room.

ACKNOWLEDGEMENTS

A very large thank-you to my husband, Andrew, for encouraging – without nagging. You are a gem. To my dear friends, Janice Wells, Lorri Neilsen Glenn and Susan Rendell, thank-you so much for reminding me that I am a writer when I (often) forget.

For their kind words, I would like to thank Stan Dragland, Lisa Moore, Janice Wells and Michael Winter. To Marnie Parsons – the best editor – you made the process delightful and painless. Thank-you.

Bless you, Newfoundland and Labrador Arts Council, for having the faith to invest in my work.

I love my characters – thanks for getting into my head and insisting that I write you.

ALSO AVAILABLE

What If Your Mom Made Raisin Buns?
ISBN-13: 978-1-897174-03-6

○○○

Bishop's Road
ISBN-13: 978-1-894294-78-2

ABOUT THE AUTHOR

Catherine Hogan Safer was born in Newfoundland's Codroy Valley and raised in Gander. Over the years she has been a waitress, bartender, flight attendant, real estate agent, restaurant manager, book promoter and on and on. She prefers writing, painting and gardening to any of those, though the money is not as good.

Her work has been well-received. Bishop's Road was short-listed for the Amazon.ca/Books in Canada first novel award. What if Your Mom Made Raisin Buns? was short-listed for the Newfoundland and Labrador Book Award and won the Marianna Dempster Award in Nova Scotia.

Catherine is not a prolific writer. She has to be in the mood. She took up painting two years ago in the hope that her muse might be hanging about the acrylics. She wasn't, although the writing has become a little more abstract. Catherine lives in St. John's, Newfoundland, a marvelous terrible place which she adores and despises in equal measure.